ARTHUR L. TAYLOR

DARK HEARTS IRON HANDS

THE CONSPIRACY

DARK HEARTS IRON HANDS

Dark Hearts Iron Hands

Published by Elite Scribes Book Writing

ISBN: 979-8-89397-322-8

Taylor vs. Management Training Cooperation: A Battle for Justice

In the hallowed halls of the United States Court for the Western District of Texas, a David-versus-Goliath battle unfolded. This was the case of *Taylor v. Management Training Corporation* (dba Gary Job Corps Center). At the heart of this legal showdown was Taylor, a determined and courageous woman who stood up against the injustices she faced in her workplace.

Taylor, who had dedicated years of service to the organization, found herself unceremoniously terminated from her position. She believed, with every fiber of her being, that this act was not a mere coincidence or the result of poor performance but a grievous violation rooted in racial discrimination. Her dismissal echoed a dark chapter in the annals of employment practices, where race still played an insidious role.

Armed with a resolute belief in the principles of equality and justice, Taylor invoked the protections afforded by 42 U.S.C. § 1981 and Title VII of the Civil Rights Act of 1964. These powerful statutes were designed to shield individuals from discrimination based on race, ensuring that all citizens could enjoy the same rights and opportunities.

The courtroom became a battleground where Taylor's voice, representing countless others who had suffered in silence, clashed against the might of the Management Training Corporation. Her case was not just a fight for personal vindication but a significant stand against systemic racial injustices in the workplace.

As the gavel struck, signaling the start of the proceedings, the story of *Taylor v. Management Training Corporation* was set in motion—a narrative of resilience, courage, and the relentless pursuit of justice that would inspire many to come.

DEDICATION

Mrs. Geraldine Williams Taylor, an individual whose unwavering commitment to the pursuit of justice and equality serves as a beacon of hope in a society often marred by inequity, deserves profound recognition for the implications of her experiences. The blatant disrespect, discrimination, and abuse she endured while employed by those in positions of power not only reflect a systemic failure to uphold ethical standards but also underscore the urgent need for reform within the job market.

Such injustices, perpetrated by individuals capable of inflicting significant harm without justification, highlight the necessity for a collective movement toward greater awareness and accountability. The examination of these issues sheds light not only on the personal ramifications for victims like Mrs. Taylor but also on the broader societal structures that perpetuate such inequities.

Gary Job Corps Center – "Where It All Began"

At Gary Job Corps Center, countless young individuals have embarked on transformative journeys since its inception. As a cornerstone of career training and personal development, this institution has empowered students to overcome challenges, gain valuable skills, and secure brighter futures. With a legacy of fostering resilience and success, Gary Job Corps Center continues to be a beacon of opportunity and hope, shaping lives and communities for the better.

TABLE OF CONTENTS

PREFACE

In an era where the principles of equality and justice are at the forefront of societal change, the case of *Taylor v. Management Training* stands as a critical examination of workplace discrimination and civil rights. This landmark case underscores the ongoing challenges faced by individuals striving for fair treatment in professional environments and highlights the legal complexities involved in addressing such issues.

Taylor v. Management Training delves into the heart of civil rights within the workplace, exploring allegations of discrimination that have far-reaching implications for both employers and employees. The case serves not only as a legal precedent but also as a narrative of resilience and the quest for justice. Through the experiences of the individuals involved, we gain insight into the systemic barriers that still exist and the efforts required to dismantle them.

This preface sets the stage for an in-depth analysis of the case, offering readers a comprehensive understanding of the facts, legal arguments, and outcomes that define *Taylor v. Management Training*. It is our hope that this examination will contribute to ongoing discussions about workplace equity, inspire further advancements in civil rights protections, and ultimately foster a more inclusive and fair professional landscape for all.

FOREWORD

The case of *Taylor v. Management Training* is more than just a legal battle; it is a powerful reminder of the ongoing struggle for civil rights and equity in the workplace. In an age where diversity and inclusion are being rightfully championed, this case highlights the real-life challenges and the resilience of those who stand against discrimination.

In this pivotal case, we witness the intersection of law, personal courage, and the pursuit of justice. *Taylor v. Management Training* not only sheds light on the systemic issues that persist in professional environments but also underscores the importance of legal frameworks designed to protect individuals from discrimination. This case is a testament to the progress we have made and the work that still lies ahead.

As you delve into the details of this case, you will gain a deeper understanding of the complexities involved in addressing workplace discrimination. The legal arguments presented, the testimonies given, and the final outcomes serve as valuable lessons for employers, employees, and policymakers alike.

CHAPTER ONE: INTRODUCTION

UNDERSTANDING DISCRIMINATION: A CONCEPTUAL FRAMEWORK

Discrimination can be defined as the unjust or prejudicial treatment of individuals based on their perceived characteristics, which may include but are not limited to race, gender, age, sexual orientation, and disability.

This phenomenon is not merely an individual act of bias; it is often entrenched within societal norms and institutional practices that perpetuate inequality. The ramifications of discrimination are far-reaching, affecting not only the individuals who are directly targeted but also the broader social fabric, leading to systemic inequities that hinder progress and cohesion.

For instance, when certain groups are consistently marginalized, their contributions to society are overlooked, which can stifle innovation and cultural enrichment. The psychological toll of discrimination is significant, manifesting in various forms of mental distress, including anxiety, depression, and diminished self-esteem. Victims of discrimination often experience a sense of alienation and disempowerment, which can lead to a withdrawal from social interactions and civic engagement.

This withdrawal affects the individual and weakens community bonds as shared experiences and collective resilience are diminished. Furthermore, the social implications of discrimination are equally concerning; communities that are marginalized due to systemic bias may struggle with economic disadvantages, limited access to education, and reduced opportunities for advancement. Consequently, the cycle of poverty and disenfranchisement is perpetuated, creating a chasm between different societal groups. This cycle can lead to intergenerational trauma, where the effects of discrimination are passed down, affecting the mental health and opportunities of future generations.

In the context of the American legal system, the Constitution serves as a foundational document that enshrines the principles of equality and justice. The rule of law ensures that all individuals are afforded the same rights and protections regardless of background. However, the effectiveness of this legal framework is contingent upon its implementation and the willingness of those in positions of power to uphold these ideals. The judicial process must be viewed as an insurance policy that safeguards civil rights against violations, mainly when discriminatory practices are perpetuated by those who wield authority.

Moreover, the legal system must evolve to address contemporary forms of discrimination, such as those based on gender identity or sexual orientation, which have historically been overlooked. This evolution requires legislative changes and a cultural shift within the legal community to recognize and combat biases that may influence judicial outcomes.

The struggle for civil rights in the United States has a rich and complex history, marked by significant milestones that reflect the ongoing battle against discrimination. From the abolition of slavery to the Civil Rights Movement of the 1960s, each era has contributed to the evolving understanding of equality and justice. Landmark legislation, such as the Civil Rights Act of 1964 and the Americans with Disabilities Act of 1990, exemplifies the legislative efforts to dismantle systemic discrimination.

Nevertheless, despite these advancements, the persistence of discriminatory practices underscores the need for continued vigilance and reform within the legal system. The historical context also highlights the importance of grassroots activism, as many of the rights enjoyed today were hard-won through the tireless efforts of individuals and organizations dedicated to social justice. Understanding this history is crucial for recognizing the ongoing struggles faced by marginalized communities and the need for sustained advocacy.

In contemporary society, discrimination manifests in various forms, including but not limited to racial profiling, gender-based wage disparities, and systemic barriers to healthcare and education. The rise of social media has amplified awareness of these issues, providing a platform for marginalized voices to be heard. However, it has also led to misinformation and divisive rhetoric that can exacerbate tensions.

The challenge lies in fostering a culture of understanding and empathy, where individuals are encouraged to confront their biases and engage in constructive dialogue. This requires individual reflection and institutional changes that promote inclusivity and diversity in all spheres of life, from workplaces to educational institutions.

Additionally, the intersectionality of discrimination must be acknowledged, as individuals may face multiple forms of bias simultaneously, complicating their experiences and the solutions needed to address them.

The Importance of Advocacy and Activism

Advocacy and activism are crucial in challenging discriminatory practices and promoting social justice. Grassroots movements, such as Black Lives Matter and the Women's March, have galvanized public support and brought attention to pressing issues of inequality. These movements underscore the importance of collective action in effecting change, as they mobilize individuals to demand accountability from those in power.

Furthermore, advocacy efforts must extend beyond the streets; engaging with policymakers and influencing legislation is essential to creating a more equitable society. This engagement can take many forms, including lobbying for policy changes, participating in public forums, and utilizing social media to raise awareness. The role of allies in these movements is also vital, as they can amplify marginalized voices and help bridge divides within communities.

However, education is a tool for change. Educational institutions can equip individuals with the knowledge and skills necessary to challenge discriminatory practices by promoting awareness of historical injustices and encouraging critical thinking. Furthermore, curricula emphasizing diversity and inclusion can help cultivate empathy and understanding among students, fostering a generation that values equality and justice.

Educational initiatives must be supported by policies that ensure equitable access to quality education for all individuals, regardless of their background. This includes addressing disparities in funding for schools in marginalized communities and implementing programs that support underrepresented students. Additionally, teacher training programs should incorporate anti-bias education to prepare educators to create inclusive classrooms that celebrate diversity.

The Path Forward

The assertion that discrimination hurts no matter who does it serves as a poignant reminder of the pervasive nature of injustice in society. While the American legal system provides a framework for addressing these issues, individuals and communities must remain vigilant in pursuing equality. The journey toward a more just society requires a collective commitment to advocacy, education, and systemic reform. By fostering a culture of respect and understanding, we can work towards a future where discrimination is acknowledged and actively dismantled, ensuring everyone is treated with dignity and respect under the rule of law.

CHAPTER TWO: FOUNDATIONAL CONTEXT

In the context of personal narratives, the journey of individuals often encapsulates not only their aspirations but also the myriad challenges they encounter along the way. The story of Geraldine and Arthur Taylor, a newly married couple, serves as a poignant illustration of this phenomenon, particularly as they navigated the complexities of relocating to a small, seemingly stagnant town in pursuit of higher education and stable employment. Their experience is emblematic of the struggles faced by many young couples who find themselves at the intersection of ambition and reality, seeking to carve out a meaningful existence in an environment that appears to offer little in terms of opportunity. This narrative not only highlights their personal growth but also reflects broader themes of resilience, community, and the pursuit of dreams against the odds.

Initial Employment: A Step Towards Stability

It was during their time in Brenham that a pivotal moment occurred, instigated by a close friend and the best man at their wedding. This individual, recognizing the couple's potential and aspirations, introduced them to the Gary Job Corps Program. His insistence that they apply for positions at the center was not merely a suggestion; it was a call to action that resonated deeply with Geraldine and Arthur. The prospect of working in a program dedicated to empowering young individuals through education and vocational training aligned perfectly with their values and aspirations. This connection not only opened doors for them but also highlighted the importance of networking and support systems in achieving one's goals.

Consequently, the couple took the leap of faith and submitted their applications, fully aware that this decision could significantly alter the trajectory of their lives. The application process itself was fraught with uncertainty, yet it also served as a testament to their commitment to personal and professional growth. The anticipation of potential employment at the Job Corps Center ignited a renewed sense of purpose within them, as they envisioned the possibility of contributing to a cause greater than themselves. This moment marked a turning point, as they began to see their aspirations not just as dreams but as attainable goals that could be realized through hard work and dedication.

A Catalyst for Change

Upon their arrival in San Marcos, the Taylors quickly sought employment opportunities, which led them to the Gary Job Corps Center. This institution, designed to provide vocational training and educational resources to young individuals, represented a beacon of hope for the couple. Geraldine's initial role as an aide at the Sweetbriar Nursing Home was particularly significant, as it not only provided her with a source of income but also allowed her to reconnect with her husband, Arthur, who was also employed at the same facility. This dual employment created a unique dynamic in their relationship, as they shared both the challenges and triumphs of their work lives.

The dynamics of working together in a nursing home setting fostered a unique bond between Geraldine and Arthur, as they navigated the challenges of their respective roles while supporting one another. This shared experience not only strengthened their relationship but also deepened their understanding of the importance of community service and the impact they could have on the lives of others. The nursing home environment, characterized by its emotional complexities and the diverse needs of its residents, offered both challenges and rewards, ultimately shaping their perspectives on life and work. They learned to appreciate the fragility of life and the importance of compassion, which would later influence their approach to their careers and community involvement.

Geraldine and Arthur's decision to relocate to San Marcos, Texas, was not made lightly; rather, it was a calculated response to their pressing need for a better quality of life. The couple was acutely aware of the importance of securing stable employment and finding a decent place to live, factors that were paramount in their decision-making process.

Brenham, Texas, characterized by its quaint charm and a palpable sense of community, presented itself as a double-edged sword. On the one hand, it offered a serene environment conducive to personal growth; on the other, it appeared to be a place where progress had stagnated, with few signs of development or economic vitality. The town's primitive nature, marked by a lack of modern amenities and infrastructure, posed significant challenges for the Taylors. The limited access to resources such as healthcare, education, and recreational facilities made their transition even more daunting.

However, the couple's determination to succeed in this new environment was unwavering. They recognized that the path to achieving their goals would require not only resilience but also a willingness to embrace the unknown. This mindset would ultimately serve as a catalyst for their personal and professional growth, pushing them to adapt and innovate in the face of adversity.

CHAPTER THREE: A JOURNEY OF TRANSFORMATION

In January of 1977, the Taylors received the news they had been eagerly awaiting—they were offered positions at the Gary Job Corps Center. This opportunity marked a significant turning point in their lives, as it not only provided them with stable employment but also allowed them to engage with a diverse population of young individuals seeking to improve their circumstances.

The center became a microcosm of hope and ambition, where the Taylors could witness firsthand the transformative power of education and vocational training. They quickly realized that their roles would not only involve teaching and mentoring but also learning from the students they served.

As they settled into their new roles, Geraldine and Arthur quickly recognized that their work at the Job Corps Center would require them to adapt to a dynamic and often challenging environment. The center's mission to empower young individuals through education and skill development resonated deeply with their own experiences, as they, too, were navigating the complexities of adulthood and the pursuit of their dreams.

This shared journey fostered a sense of camaraderie among the staff and the students, creating an atmosphere of mutual support and encouragement. They found themselves inspired by the resilience of the young people they worked with, which further fueled their passion for their roles.

Challenges and Triumphs: Navigating the Job Corps Experience

While the opportunity at the Gary Job Corps Center was undoubtedly a blessing, it was not without its challenges. The couple faced numerous obstacles as they endeavored to balance their professional responsibilities with their personal lives.

The demands of their jobs, coupled with the pressures of adapting to a new community, often left them feeling overwhelmed. The emotional toll of working in a setting that dealt with the struggles of at-risk youth was significant, and they often found themselves grappling with feelings of inadequacy and self-doubt. *Are we truly making a difference?* Geraldine often wondered.

However, it was precisely in these moments of adversity that their resilience and determination were put to the test. Through perseverance and a commitment to their goals, Geraldine and Arthur gradually began to find their footing within the community.

They forged meaningful connections with their colleagues and the young individuals they served, fostering an environment of trust and collaboration. The sense of fulfillment derived from witnessing the growth and development of their students served as a powerful motivator, reinforcing their belief in the importance of education and the potential for positive change.

They celebrated small victories, such as a student graduating or securing a job, which reminded them of the impact they were making on the lives of others. *These moments make it all worth it,* Arthur reflected during one particularly gratifying graduation ceremony.

Reflections on Growth and Development

As the Taylors continued their journey in Brenham, they began to reflect on the profound impact that their experiences had on their personal and professional growth. The challenges they faced, while daunting, ultimately served as catalysts for self-discovery and resilience.

They learned to navigate the complexities of their new environment, embracing the opportunities for growth that arose from their experiences at the Gary Job Corps Center. This period of reflection allowed them to appreciate the lessons learned and the strengths they had developed as a couple.

Through perseverance and a commitment to their goals, Geraldine and Arthur gradually began to find their footing within the community. They forged meaningful connections with their colleagues and the young individuals they served, fostering an environment of trust and collaboration. The sense of fulfillment derived from witnessing the growth and development of their students served as a powerful motivator, reinforcing their belief in the importance of education and the potential for positive change.

They celebrated small victories, such as a student graduating or securing a job, which reminded them of the impact they were making in the lives of others. Moreover, their time in Brenham, Texas, allowed them to cultivate a deeper understanding of the importance of community engagement and social responsibility. The couple recognized that their roles at the Job Corps Center extended beyond mere employment; they were part of a larger movement aimed at empowering individuals to achieve their goals and realize their potential.

This realization instilled in them a profound sense of purpose, motivating them to continue their work with dedication and passion. They became advocates for their students, often going above and beyond to ensure that everyone received the support they needed to succeed.

The initial excitement of the new role quickly gave way to the harsh realities of their day-to-day responsibilities. Each day presented new hurdles, from navigating bureaucratic red tape to addressing the immediate needs of the youth they served. Their personal lives suffered as well, with long hours at the center encroaching on time that could have been spent fostering their own relationship and well-being. *Are we doing enough?* Geraldine often wondered, her thoughts swirling during sleepless nights.

Despite the exhaustion and emotional drain, the couple discovered a deeper strength within themselves. Their shared commitment to making a difference became a source of mutual support and motivation. They began to find innovative ways to manage their workload, creating new programs and outreach strategies that better addressed the needs of the youth. Through these efforts, they not only helped to transform the lives of those they served but also reinforced their own sense of purpose and partnership.

Their journey was marked by moments of doubt and struggle, but it also brought about profound personal growth. They learned to lean on each other and to draw strength from their shared mission, finding that their greatest achievements often came from their darkest times. In the end, the challenges they faced only solidified their resolve and demonstrated the true depth of their commitment to their work and to each other.

As time went on, they became integral parts of the community, known not only for their dedication and hard work but also for their unwavering support for the students' dreams and aspirations. Geraldine's empathetic approach and Arthur's practical problem-solving skills complemented each other perfectly, creating a holistic support system for the youth under their care.

They also sought to engage with the larger community, organizing events that brought together students, their families, and local residents. These gatherings fostered a sense of unity and shared purpose, bridging gaps and building bridges of understanding and cooperation. Geraldine and Arthur's tireless efforts began to pay off as they saw firsthand the transformation in their students, who were not only achieving academically but also growing into confident, capable, and hopeful individuals.

Through it all, they remained grounded and humble, aware that their journey was as much about learning and growing as it was about teaching and guiding. Each challenge they overcame and every success they celebrated deepened their commitment to their work and to each other. Their story became an inspiring testament to the power of resilience, compassion, and unwavering dedication to making a difference in the lives of those around them.

As the Taylors continued their journey in San Marcos, they began to reflect on the profound impact that their experiences had on their personal and professional growth. The challenges they faced, while daunting, ultimately served as catalysts for self-discovery and resilience. They learned to navigate the complexities of their new environment, embracing the opportunities for growth that arose from their experiences at the Gary Job Corps Center.

This period of reflection allowed them to appreciate the lessons learned and the strengths they had developed as a couple. Their time at the Gary Job Corps Center became a defining chapter in their lives, one that shaped their identities and future paths. The bonds they forged and the positive changes they witnessed in their students reinforced their belief in the power of education and mentorship.

They also realized the importance of community and the profound impact that a supportive network can have on both personal and professional development. This understanding guided their actions and decisions as they continued to contribute to their new community.

In reflecting on their journey, Geraldine and Arthur acknowledged the importance of perseverance and adaptability in overcoming adversity. They found that their experiences had not only made them stronger individuals but also a more resilient and united couple. Their shared commitment to their goals and their ability to support each other through challenging times became the cornerstone of their success. As they looked to the future, they carried with them the lessons learned and the determination to continue making a positive impact wherever their path might lead.

CHAPTER FOUR: CULTIVATING COMMUNITY ENGAGEMENT AND SOCIAL RESPONSIBILITY

Their time in San Marcos allowed Geraldine and Arthur to cultivate a deeper understanding of the significance of community engagement and social responsibility. Immersed in the vibrant and diverse community, they came to appreciate the interconnectedness of their efforts with the well-being and growth of those around them. They recognized that their roles at the Job Corps Center extended beyond mere employment; they were part of a larger movement aimed at empowering individuals to achieve their goals and realize their potential.

This realization instilled in them a profound sense of purpose, motivating them to continue their work with unwavering dedication and passion. Each day, they witnessed the transformative power of education and support as students began to believe in their capabilities and aspire to greater heights. Geraldine and Arthur became ardent advocates for their students, understanding that their success was intertwined with the future prosperity of the entire community.

Their commitment went far beyond the confines of their job descriptions. They tirelessly sought out resources, opportunities, and networks that could benefit their students. Whether it was arranging internships or providing personal mentorship, they often went above and beyond to ensure that everyone received the support they needed to succeed. They meticulously researched and connected with local businesses, educational institutions, and charitable organizations to create a robust support system for their students. Geraldine and Arthur understood that these connections could open doors to a brighter future for many young individuals, fostering hope and ambition.

They organized on-campus community events, workshops, and support groups, fostering a sense of belonging and collective progress. These gatherings became a cornerstone of their approach, offering a platform for students to share their experiences, challenges, and successes. The couple worked diligently to create an inclusive environment where every student felt valued and heard. They brought in guest speakers, coordinated career fairs, and facilitated skill-building workshops that equipped students with the knowledge and confidence to pursue their goals.

Their efforts did not go unnoticed. They garnered respect and admiration from colleagues, students, and community members alike. The trust they built created an environment where students felt safe and encouraged to pursue their dreams. Geraldine and Arthur's passion was contagious, inspiring others to contribute and get involved, further strengthening the fabric of the community. Their dedication inspired a culture of mutual support and collective progress, where everyone was invested in the success of the youth.

In this journey, Geraldine and Arthur found their own personal growth. The challenges they faced and the victories they celebrated deepened their understanding of what it means to serve and lead. They learned to navigate complex social dynamics, mediate conflicts, and build bridges between diverse groups. Their experiences in Brenham became a testament to the power of resilience, compassion, and unwavering dedication to the betterment of others. *True leadership is about empowering others, lifting them up, and creating opportunities for them to shine,* Geraldine reflected.

Through their unwavering commitment and tireless efforts, Geraldine and Arthur not only transformed the lives of their students but also left an indelible mark on the community. Their legacy was one of hope, inspiration, and profound positive change, demonstrating the remarkable impact that dedicated individuals can have when they are driven by a sense of purpose and compassion.

Final Thoughts

The journey of Geraldine and Arthur Taylor serves as a testament to the power of resilience, determination, and community engagement. Their decision to relocate to Brenham, Texas, in pursuit of higher education and stable employment was fraught with challenges, yet it ultimately led to profound personal and professional growth. Through their experiences at the Gary Job Corps Center, they not only contributed to the empowerment of young individuals but also discovered their own capacity for transformation.

Their story is a reminder that the path to success is rarely linear and that the struggles faced can lead to unexpected opportunities for growth. It underscores the significance of embracing change and recognizing the potential for growth within challenges. *The struggles we face today build the strength we need for tomorrow,* Arthur often mused during moments of reflection.

As they continue to navigate their journey, the Taylors remain steadfast in their aspirations, driven by the belief that their experiences have equipped them with the tools necessary to succeed in an ever-evolving world. Ultimately, their narrative serves as an inspiration for others who find themselves at the crossroads of ambition and reality, reminding everyone of the transformative power of perseverance and community. Their journey is not just a personal tale but a universal message about the importance of hope, hard work, and the connections forged along the way.

The job at Gary did not come without growing pains or job stresses, but it ultimately shaped them into more resilient and determined individuals, ready to face whatever the future holds.

CHAPTER FIVE: A CATALYST FOR BURNOUT

Burnout, a term that has gained significant traction in contemporary discourse—particularly within the realms of psychology and organizational behavior—refers to a state of chronic physical and emotional exhaustion, often precipitated by prolonged exposure to stressors in the workplace. The case of Geraldine Taylor, who experienced burnout from April 2004 through November 2005, serves as a poignant illustration of the detrimental effects that excessive stress, emotional exhaustion, and depersonalization can have on an individual's professional and personal life. This story explores the multifaceted dimensions of burnout, particularly in the context of Taylor's experiences at the Gary Job Corps Center, operated by the Management Training Corporation (MTC), one of the largest private federal government contractors for the United States Department of Labor.

The examination encompasses the underlying causes of Taylor's burnout, the role of management in exacerbating the situation, and the broader implications for organizational practices and employee well-being.

To fully comprehend the phenomenon of burnout, it is essential to delineate its core components. Burnout is characterized by three primary dimensions: emotional exhaustion, personality traits, and a diminished sense of personal accomplishment. Emotional exhaustion manifests as a pervasive feeling of fatigue and depletion, often leading to a sense of being overwhelmed by the demands of one's job. Depersonalization, on the other hand, involves a detachment from one's work and the people one serves, often resulting in a cynical attitude toward colleagues and clients. Finally, a diminished sense of personal accomplishment refers to the feelings of ineffectiveness and lack of achievement that can accompany burnout. Understanding these dimensions is crucial for recognizing the signs of burnout early and implementing effective interventions.

Geraldine Taylor's experience of burnout was not an isolated incident but rather a culmination of systemic issues within the organizational structure of the Gary Job Corps Center. The Wellness Center Management, tasked with overseeing the health and well-being of employees, failed to adequately address the mounting stressors that contributed to Taylor's deteriorating mental health. The lack of intervention from senior management regarding numerous complaints related to employment discrimination further exacerbated the situation, creating an environment rife with tension and dissatisfaction. This neglect not only affected Taylor but also had a ripple effect on her colleagues, leading to a pervasive atmosphere of discontent and disengagement among staff members.

In Taylor's case, excessive stress was a significant catalyst for her burnout. The demands of her role, compounded by the lack of support from management, created a perfect storm of stressors that ultimately led to her emotional exhaustion. Research indicates that high levels of job demand, coupled with low levels of control, can significantly increase the risk of burnout. In Taylor's situation, the absence of autonomy in her work, combined with the relentless pressures of her responsibilities, contributed to her feelings of being overwhelmed and powerless. This lack of control not only diminished her job satisfaction but also eroded her confidence in her professional abilities, further fueling her burnout.

Burnout – Stress

Emotional Exhaustion Took a Toll on Mental Health

Emotional exhaustion, a phenomenon that has garnered increasing attention in contemporary psychological discourse, is characterized by a profound sense of fatigue that transcends mere physical tiredness. This state of depletion encompasses not only the physical but also the emotional and psychological resources of individuals, rendering them incapable of effectively meeting the demands imposed by their professional and personal roles.

In Taylor's case, continuous exposure to various stressors without adequate support mechanisms culminated in a debilitating state of emotional depletion. *How much longer can I keep this up?* she wondered as the demands of her role became increasingly unmanageable.

Exploring the implications of emotional exhaustion highlights its effects on professional performance, personal relationships, and the psychological defense mechanisms that may arise as a consequence.

The Impact of Emotional Exhaustion on Professional Performance

Emotional exhaustion manifests in various ways within the professional realm, often leading to a significant decline in performance and productivity. Individuals experiencing this condition may find themselves unable to concentrate, resulting in diminished cognitive function and impaired decision-making abilities. In Taylor's situation, the relentless demands of her job, coupled with insufficient support from colleagues and management, contributed to her emotional fatigue. Consequently, her ability to engage with her work diminished, leading to a cycle of decreased motivation and increased absenteeism. Furthermore, the quality of her output suffered, as the emotional toll of her exhaustion overshadowed her professional capabilities. This decline not only affected Taylor but also disrupted team dynamics and overall workplace morale.

Emotional Exhaustion and Personal Relationships

The ramifications of emotional exhaustion extend far beyond the confines of the workplace, often permeating an individual's personal life and interpersonal relationships. Friends and family members observed notable changes in her behavior, such as increased irritability, withdrawal from social interactions, and a general sense of disengagement. Taylor's emotional depletion manifested in strained relationships with loved ones, as her capacity for empathy and connection diminished. The emotional resources required to maintain healthy relationships were depleted, leading to feelings of isolation and loneliness. This withdrawal created a vicious cycle, leaving her increasingly disconnected from her support system and exacerbating her feelings of exhaustion and despair.

Defense Mechanisms: Depersonalization as a Response to Burnout

In the face of overwhelming emotional exhaustion, individuals may resort to various psychological defense mechanisms as a means of coping with the emotional toll of their circumstances. One such mechanism is depersonalization, which allows individuals to create a psychological distance from the emotional burdens associated with their work. This phenomenon can serve as a temporary respite, enabling individuals to navigate their professional responsibilities without becoming overwhelmed by the emotional weight of their experiences. However, while depersonalization may provide short-term relief, it can also lead to long-term consequences, including further erosion of emotional connections and an inability to engage authentically with colleagues and loved ones. In Taylor's case, this reliance on depersonalization initially appeared to be a viable coping strategy but eventually contributed to a profound sense of disconnection and alienation from her emotional landscape.

Conclusion: The Need for Comprehensive Support Systems

In summary, emotional exhaustion represents a multifaceted challenge that significantly impacts both professional performance and personal relationships. Taylor's experience illustrates the profound effects of continuous exposure to stressors without adequate support, leading to a state of emotional depletion that permeates various aspects of life. The implications of emotional exhaustion underscore the necessity for organizations to implement comprehensive support systems that prioritize employee well-being, fostering an environment conducive to emotional resilience.

Recognizing the psychological defense mechanisms that may arise in response to burnout is crucial for developing effective interventions. By addressing the root causes of emotional exhaustion and promoting a culture of support and understanding, individuals can be empowered to reclaim their emotional resources, ultimately enhancing both their professional and personal lives.

CHAPTER SIX: EMPLOYMENT DISCRIMINATION: A CONTRIBUTING FACTOR

Employment discrimination, as highlighted in Taylor's experience, serves as a significant stressor that exacerbates feelings of burnout. Discrimination in the workplace manifests in various forms, including unequal treatment, lack of opportunities for advancement, and hostile work environments. The psychological toll of such experiences leads to heightened stress levels, emotional exhaustion, and, ultimately, burnout. Taylor's situation underscores the importance of addressing discrimination not only as a legal and ethical obligation but also as a critical component of fostering a healthy work environment. Organizations must implement robust policies and training programs to promote diversity, equity, and inclusion, ensuring that all employees feel valued and supported.

Implications for Organizational Practices

The implications of Taylor's experience highlight the importance of organizations prioritizing employee well-being as a core aspect of their operations. Recognizing that employee health is directly tied to overall productivity and success, companies should adopt comprehensive wellness programs, encourage open communication, and foster a culture of inclusivity. Regular evaluations of workplace culture and employee satisfaction can help identify areas for improvement and address potential issues proactively, reducing the risk of burnout and ensuring a supportive work environment.

To effectively combat burnout, organizations must adopt a multifaceted approach that encompasses both prevention and intervention strategies. Preventive measures include regular assessments of employee workload, the establishment of support systems, and the promotion of work-life balance. Additionally, training programs aimed at enhancing managerial skills in recognizing and addressing burnout empower leaders to create more supportive work environments.

During the case of *Taylor v. Management Training,* Taylor's mental state had to be considered by her representing attorney in case it became an issue at trial. Several factors were established to play a part in the potential settlement of her case. Burnout, a psychological syndrome characterized by emotional exhaustion, depersonalization, and a diminished sense of personal accomplishment, has emerged as a significant concern in contemporary work environments. This phenomenon is particularly pronounced among individuals who experience chronic stressors, including workplace discrimination, which exacerbates feelings of isolation and inadequacy.

In Geraldine's case, facing such adversities made it imperative to implement targeted interventions to facilitate her recovery and reintegration into a healthier work environment. *This story will explore the necessity of counseling services, professional development opportunities, and the establishment of peer support networks as essential components in addressing burnout and fostering resilience.*

The provision of counseling services represents a critical intervention for individuals experiencing burnout. Such services offer a safe space for individuals like Geraldine to articulate their feelings and experiences, facilitating emotional processing and cognitive restructuring. Through therapeutic engagement, individuals develop coping strategies tailored to their unique circumstances, particularly in the context of workplace discrimination. Furthermore, counseling assists in identifying maladaptive thought patterns that contribute to feelings of inadequacy and helplessness, allowing for the cultivation of a more nuanced understanding of one's professional identity and worth. Consequently, the integration of counseling services within organizational frameworks not only addresses the immediate psychological needs of employees but also promotes long-term well-being and productivity.

In addition to counseling, the provision of professional development opportunities is paramount in empowering individuals to reclaim their autonomy and sense of agency within the workplace. Such opportunities may include skills training, mentorship programs, and leadership workshops, all of which enhance an individual's competencies and confidence. For Geraldine, engaging in professional development mitigates feelings of stagnation and inadequacy that often accompany burnout, particularly when exacerbated by discriminatory practices. By fostering an environment that prioritizes continuous learning and growth, organizations not only enhance employee satisfaction but also cultivate a culture of inclusivity and support. This proactive approach aids in recovery from burnout and serves as a preventive measure against future occurrences.

The establishment of peer support networks is another vital component in combating burnout, particularly in the context of shared experiences related to workplace discrimination. These networks facilitate the creation of a sense of community, wherein individuals share their challenges and triumphs, fostering a culture of mutual understanding and support. For Geraldine, connecting with peers who have faced similar adversities significantly alleviates feelings of isolation and alienation, which are often exacerbated by the stigma associated with burnout. Furthermore, peer support networks serve as a platform for collective advocacy, empowering individuals to address systemic issues within the workplace that contribute to burnout. By promoting solidarity and shared resilience, these networks play a pivotal role in the recovery process.

Addressing burnout, particularly in individuals like Geraldine who have experienced workplace discrimination, necessitates a multifaceted approach that encompasses counseling services, professional development opportunities, and the establishment of peer support networks. These interventions not only provide immediate relief from the psychological distress associated with burnout but also foster a culture of resilience and inclusivity within the workplace. As organizations increasingly recognize the profound implications of burnout on employee well-being and productivity, implementing such targeted interventions becomes not merely beneficial but essential. By prioritizing the mental health and professional development of employees, organizations cultivate a more engaged, satisfied, and productive workforce, thereby mitigating the pervasive effects of burnout in contemporary work environments.

The case of Geraldine Taylor serves as a compelling reminder of the profound impact burnout has on individuals and organizations alike. Burnout, characterized by excessive stress, emotional exhaustion, and depersonalization, emerges as a significant concern in contemporary work environments. This phenomenon affects not only an individual's mental and physical health but also reverberates throughout the organizational structure, leading to decreased productivity, increased absenteeism, and a detrimental workplace culture. Consequently, it is imperative to explore the multifaceted nature of burnout, its implications, and the necessary interventions that organizations must adopt to foster a healthier work environment.

Training programs aimed at enhancing managerial skills in recognizing and addressing burnout empower leaders to create supportive environments. In addition, fostering a culture of resilience through team-building activities and stress management workshops significantly reduces the likelihood of burnout among employees. These strategies address the immediate symptoms of burnout and contribute to a long-term shift in organizational culture, promoting a more compassionate and understanding workplace.

The Implications of Taylor's Experience

Ultimately, the lessons learned from Geraldine Taylor's experience serve as a catalyst for change within organizations. By acknowledging the profound impact of burnout on both individuals and the organization as a whole, leaders can take proactive steps to create a healthier work environment. The recognition that a healthy workforce is essential for sustained success cannot be overstated. Organizations that prioritize employee well-being are more likely to experience higher levels of engagement, productivity, and retention. Furthermore, addressing systemic issues related to workplace stress and discrimination benefits employees and enhances the organization's reputation and competitiveness in the market.

Conclusion

The case of Geraldine Taylor underscores the critical importance of addressing burnout within the modern workplace. The interplay of excessive stress, emotional exhaustion, and inadequate management responses leads to significant consequences for both individuals and organizations. By fostering supportive environments, addressing systemic issues, and implementing effective prevention and intervention strategies, organizations can mitigate the risk of burnout and promote a culture of resilience and well-being. As the complexities of the modern workplace continue to evolve, it is imperative that organizations remain vigilant in their efforts to prioritize employee health, ultimately leading to a more productive and harmonious work environment.

CHAPTER SEVEN: TAYLOR EEOC COMPLAINTS

In October 2004, a significant incident highlighted the challenges within the management practices at the MTC/Gary Job Corps Center. Geraldine Taylor, an LVN, became the center of a dispute involving a letter of concern issued by Carol Elaine Benson, the Nursing Supervisor at the Wellness Center. The letter of concern, a formal communication addressing Taylor's performance and conduct, was met with resistance and rebuttal from Taylor, who believed it was unwarranted and did not adhere to MTC's established disciplinary policies. This incident not only affected Taylor's professional standing but also raised broader questions about the center's management practices and the treatment of employees within the organization.

Disciplinary Policies at MTC

Understanding MTC's disciplinary policies is crucial to evaluating the legitimacy of the letter of concern issued to Taylor. According to MTC's progressive disciplinary policy, specific protocols must be followed when addressing employee performance issues. These protocols typically involve a series of steps, including verbal warnings, written cautions, and, if necessary, more severe disciplinary actions. The issuance of a letter of concern, as opposed to a letter of caution, raises questions about whether the proper procedures were followed in Taylor's case. The lack of adherence to these protocols undermines management's credibility and creates an environment where employees may feel insecure about their positions and uncertain about expectations.

As complaints leading to the civil action on workplace discrimination are disclosed, the reasoning and policies of MTC and the EEOC are explored in-depth to develop a prima facie case.

The Meeting of October 14, 2004

The meeting held on October 14, 2004, was a pivotal moment in this dispute. Attendees included Carol Elaine Benson, Melissa Valdez (the Human Resources Manager), and Geraldine Taylor. During the meeting, Taylor sought to address the concerns raised in Benson's letter and challenge the validity of the accusations made against her. The presence of the Human Resources Manager underscored the seriousness of the situation, as it involved not only Taylor's professional reputation but also the adherence to MTC's policies and procedures.

The discussions during the meeting were intense. Taylor presented her case, citing specific examples of her performance that contradicted the claims in the letter. This confrontation highlighted the importance of open communication and transparency in addressing employee grievances, which are essential for maintaining trust and morale within the workplace.

Rebuttal to the Letter of Concern

In her response to the letter of concern, Taylor articulated her position clearly, emphasizing that the accusations made by Benson were unfounded. She pointed out that the letter did not follow the established disciplinary procedures, which should have included a prior verbal warning or written caution. Taylor's rebuttal was not just a defense of her actions; it was also a challenge to the management practices at the center, highlighting potential failures in oversight and accountability mechanisms governing employee relations. Her response underscored the importance of due process in disciplinary actions and the need for management to be held accountable for their decisions.

Implications for Management Practices

The situation surrounding Taylor's complaint and rebuttal raises significant implications for management practices at the MTC/Gary Job Corps Center. It calls into question the effectiveness of the center's human resources policies. When employees feel subject to unwarranted disciplinary actions without due process, it fosters a toxic work environment, decreases morale, and increases turnover rates. Poor management practices not only harm individual employees but also jeopardize the center's mission to provide a supportive and educational environment for students.

Employee Rights and Protections

Protecting employee rights, particularly in matters related to disciplinary actions, is essential. Taylor's case highlights the importance of clear and transparent policies outlining procedures for addressing performance issues and providing employees with a means to contest unwarranted accusations. Without such protections, staff may feel vulnerable, leading to diminished performance and strained organizational functioning.

To address these issues, several recommendations can be made to improve management practices at MTC/Gary Job Corps Center:

- Conduct a thorough review of existing disciplinary policies to ensure they align with best practices and are consistently applied.
- Provide training for management staff on disciplinary procedures, emphasizing fairness and transparency.
- Establish a robust grievance procedure to empower employees to voice concerns without fear of retaliation, potentially through an independent committee to review complaints.

- Implement regular feedback mechanisms to gauge employee satisfaction and identify areas for improvement.

Conclusion

The case of Geraldine Taylor and the letter of concern issued by Carol Elaine Benson serves as a critical example of the challenges faced by employees within the MTC/Gary Job Corps Center. It underscores the need for adherence to established disciplinary policies and the importance of protecting employee rights in the workplace. By addressing these issues and implementing recommended improvements, the center can foster a more positive and productive work environment, benefiting both employees and students. A commitment to fair management practices enhances employee morale and contributes to the overall success of the Job Corps program, ensuring it fulfills its mission of empowering young individuals through education and vocational training.

CHAPTER EIGHT: CONTINUATION OF COMPLAINTS AND REBUTTALS

In examining the memorandum dated May 20, 2005, authored by Glenda Steen, it becomes evident that a series of actions taken by Phyllis P. Smith and her associates raise significant concerns regarding workplace ethics and potential violations of employment law. The memorandum serves as a critical piece of evidence, illustrating a pattern of behavior that undermines the principles of fairness and transparency while suggesting a deliberate attempt to manipulate personnel decisions to the detriment of Ms. Steen.

Firstly, the promotion of Barbara Garza to the position of Senior Secretary to the Health Services Administrator, without formal posting or consideration of other candidates, indicates a lack of adherence to standard hiring practices. This action not only contravenes the principles of meritocracy but also raises questions about the motivation behind such decisions. The absence of Corps experience on Ms. Garza's part exacerbates the situation, suggesting that the decision was not based on qualifications but rather on personal biases or ulterior motives.

Moreover, the memorandum highlights instances of harassment and intimidation directed toward Ms. Steen by both Mrs. Smith and Mrs. Benson. The imposition of unreasonable timelines for assignments, coupled with the unauthorized search of Ms. Steen's office, constitutes a clear violation of professional conduct and raises serious ethical concerns. Such actions not only create a hostile work environment but also reflect a broader culture of discrimination and retaliation, profoundly affecting employee morale and organizational integrity.

In addition, the involvement of Mrs. Taylor, who refused to participate in the alleged defamation efforts, underscores the complexity of the interpersonal dynamics at play within the Wellness Center. This refusal likely reflects an acknowledgment of the unethical nature of the actions pursued by Mrs. Smith, further validating Ms. Steen's claims of misconduct.

To sum up, the evidence presented in the memorandum validates Ms. Steen's prior complaints and raises serious doubts about the legitimacy of the personnel decisions made during this period. This situation goes beyond one person's grievances; it underscores the broader need for organizations to uphold ethical standards and ensure that every employee is treated with respect and fairness.

For Ms. Steen, these revelations are deeply personal. They echo the frustrations and emotional turmoil she has experienced, reaffirming the validity of her struggles. This is not just about her standing up for her rights but also about the collective responsibility of the organization to foster a culture of accountability and integrity.

The examination of this case serves as a stark reminder of the critical importance of accountability in the workplace. It highlights the necessity of robust mechanisms to address violations of employee rights, ensuring that all voices are heard and justice is served. This moment is a call to action for the organization to reflect on its practices and commit to meaningful change.

For every employee who has felt marginalized or unheard, Ms. Steen's case is a beacon of hope — a powerful testament to the significance of standing up for what is right. It highlights the necessity of fostering a workplace environment where every individual is not only valued and respected but also encouraged to voice their concerns without fear of retribution.

Ms. Steen's courage in coming forward and challenging the status quo reminds us that change begins with the bravery of a single individual willing to demand better. Her case underscores the importance of ethical conduct being more than just an expectation — it must be the bedrock of professional interactions.

This serves as a call to action for organizations to introspect and implement robust mechanisms that ensure fairness, transparency, and accountability. It is a reminder that when employees are empowered to speak out, the entire organization benefits, paving the way for a more inclusive and just workplace. Ms. Steen's journey is not just a personal victory but a catalyst for broader systemic change, inspiring others to stand up for their rights and contribute to a culture of integrity and respect.

Response and Notices: Rebuttal to Accusations Sent to Human Resource Management Training Corporation d/b/a Gary Job Corps Center

In addressing the allegations presented against the staff at the Gary Job Corps Center, it is imperative to examine the claims with a critical lens, particularly considering the systemic issues that have been reported. References to "voodoo" and the derogatory comparisons of black employees to NBA players and criminals not only reflect profound insensitivity but also suggest an underlying bias that permeates the workplace environment. Such remarks contribute to a hostile atmosphere, detrimental to both employee morale and organizational integrity.

Furthermore, the denial of vacation requests for two black employees on the 4th of July, while similar requests from Caucasian and Hispanic employees were granted, raises significant concerns regarding discriminatory practices within the management structure. This pattern of behavior indicates a broader issue of inequity that must be addressed to foster an inclusive workplace.

The issuance of a Performance Improvement Plan (PIP) against a Black employee, following complaints regarding unrealistic work assignments set by the Health Services Administrator, Francisco Pena, exemplifies a retaliatory approach that undermines the principles of fair treatment and respect. The employee in question possesses over a decade of experience at the Job Corps Wellness Center, contrasting sharply with Pena's relatively limited tenure. Such discrepancies in experience should be acknowledged rather than dismissed. Additionally, Carol Benson, RN, Nursing Supervisor, has perpetuated a hostile work environment by provoking conflicts and challenging established Job Corps procedures. Benson's lack of prior experience in Job Corps operations, coupled with her attempts to undermine the authority of seasoned staff, illustrates a troubling disregard for the expertise long-serving employees bring to the organization.

The conduct of Mary Beth Magovsky, RN, Health Services Administrator, is equally concerning. Her engagement in gossip about downline staff and subsequent denial of such behavior fosters distrust among employees and creates a toxic work culture. The accusation of theft against an employee, without substantiated evidence, further illustrates a pattern of harassment and intimidation that cannot be overlooked.

The allegations and behaviors outlined herein reflect a significant need for intervention at the Gary Job Corps Center. Human Resource Management must take these concerns seriously and implement measures to rectify the hostile work environment, ensuring that all employees are treated equitably and with the respect they deserve. Addressing these issues is not merely a matter of compliance but a fundamental requirement for fostering a healthy and productive workplace.

In addressing the troubling circumstances surrounding the actions of Ms. Smith and Ms. Benson, it is imperative to underscore the gravity of their unauthorized access to confidential files and documents. This breach of professional ethics raises significant concerns about the treatment of minority employees within the workplace. The fact that these individuals selectively targeted two Black employees for scrutiny indicates a broader pattern of discrimination that cannot be ignored.

The hostile work environment perpetuated by Ms. Smith and Ms. Benson has led to a palpable sense of distress among staff members, particularly minority employees who have courageously voiced their grievances but, in many cases, have felt compelled to resign due to pervasive harassment. The situation is exacerbated by management's apparent inaction, which has allowed the toxic atmosphere to persist unchecked, breeding a culture of fear and alienation. This neglect undermines trust and morale, signaling a troubling tolerance for unacceptable behavior.

The emotional and psychological toll on affected employees cannot be overstated. Many find themselves working in an environment where their voices are ignored, their well-being is compromised, and their professional contributions are devalued. This toxic environment stifles creativity, reduces productivity, and hampers the organization's overall progress.

Addressing this hostile work environment requires urgent and decisive action from management to implement comprehensive policies promoting inclusivity, respect, and fairness. Only by fostering an environment where every employee feels valued and protected can the organization hope to rebuild trust and ensure a healthy, productive workplace.

It is particularly disheartening that despite 27 years of extensive experience within the organization, I have been subjected to punitive measures, defamation, and humiliation by individuals lacking the requisite knowledge and experience regarding Job Corps operations. The assertion that my competence is being called into question by Ms. Smith and Ms. Benson, who have no prior affiliation with Job Corps, is unfounded and undermines the integrity of the programs I have diligently developed and managed.

The Wellness Center, which I have successfully overseen, has been recognized for its compliance with US Department of Labor standards, reflecting the effectiveness of the procedures I implemented as an Acting Health Service Administrator. The sudden shift toward non-compliance and the emergence of significant violations can be directly attributed to the disruptive influence of Ms. Smith and Ms. Benson, whose actions have unjustly marginalized my contributions and expertise. These issues must be addressed urgently to restore equity and professionalism within the workplace.

The case filing with the Equal Employment Opportunity Commission (EEOC) was predicated upon several critical assertions that underscore the complexities of employment discrimination law. The refusal to comply with an order may be justified if the individual reasonably believes the order is inherently discriminatory. This principle recognizes that an individual's refusal to obey an order constitutes protected opposition, particularly when there exists a good faith belief that compliance would necessitate participation in unlawful employment discrimination. Protection against retaliation is afforded to those who oppose perceived discriminatory practices, irrespective of whether those practices are ultimately deemed unlawful.

The legal framework surrounding retaliation is nuanced. Judicial interpretations emphasize that a definitive finding of actual illegality is not a prerequisite for establishing a violation of the retaliation provision. This perspective aligns with Title VII's overarching objective: the eradication of employment discrimination through informal mechanisms. Courts have stressed that requiring a finding of actual illegality would undermine this purpose and inhibit essential dialogue between employers and employees, which is vital for fostering a nondisruptive workplace environment.

The concept of adverse actions encompasses a broad spectrum of retaliatory behaviors that can manifest in the workplace. While conspicuous forms of retaliation include denial of promotion, refusal to hire, demotion, suspension, and termination, subtler forms such as threats, reprimands, negative performance evaluations, harassment, or other detrimental treatment also qualify. The Ninth Circuit has elucidated that the severity of harm is pertinent to the determination of damage, not liability. To substantiate a claim of unlawful retaliation, it must be demonstrated that the respondent undertook an adverse action as a direct consequence of the charging party's engagement in protected activity. This evidentiary burden can be met through direct or circumstantial evidence, reinforcing the critical nature of retaliatory motive in establishing liability.

In workplace rights and protections, the EEOC serves as a pivotal institution in addressing and rectifying instances of discrimination and employee rights violations. Established under the Civil Rights Act of 1964, the EEOC enforces federal laws prohibiting discrimination based on race, color, religion, sex, national origin, age, disability, or genetic information. Before initiating an EEOC complaint, it is imperative to explore and exhaust all available avenues for resolution within the organizational framework. Thorough documentation, effective communication with management, and establishing a clear record of grievances are critical steps before proceeding with an EEOC complaint.

CHAPTER NINE: UNDERSTANDING THE EEOC PROCESS

The EEOC is a federal agency tasked with enforcing laws against workplace discrimination. It is essential to comprehend the procedural aspects of filing a complaint with the EEOC, as well as the implications of such actions. Filing an EEOC complaint is not merely a procedural formality; it is a significant step that can have lasting repercussions on both the employee and the employer. The process typically begins with the employee filing a charge of discrimination, which the EEOC then investigates. Depending on the findings, the EEOC may issue a "right to sue" letter, allowing the employee to take legal action against the employer. Therefore, it is prudent to ensure that all internal mechanisms for conflict resolution have been adequately explored before escalating the matter to this federal level. Understanding the timeline and potential outcomes of the EEOC process helps employees make informed decisions about their next steps.

One of the most critical components in the pre-EEOC complaint process is the meticulous documentation of all relevant incidents and communications. This documentation serves multiple purposes: it provides a factual basis for the claims being made, creates a timeline of events, and demonstrates the employee's commitment to resolving the issue amicably. In the case of Delia Allen, the preparation of massive documentation on a daily basis regarding her medication issues at the wellness center exemplifies the importance of maintaining a detailed record. Such documentation should include dates, times, individuals involved, and the nature of the complaints, thereby creating a comprehensive account of the grievances. Additionally, employees should consider documenting any witnesses to the incidents, as their testimonies may prove invaluable during the investigation process. By compiling this information, employees can build a robust case that supports their claims and illustrates the severity of the situation.

Prior to filing an EEOC complaint, employees are encouraged to engage in open and constructive dialogue with their immediate supervisors or relevant management personnel. This communication should be approached with a spirit of collaboration, aiming to resolve the issues at hand without the need for external intervention. In the context of Delia Allen's situation, it would have been prudent for her to formally address her concerns regarding the lack of clarity surrounding her medication prescription with the wellness center's management. Such discussions often lead to immediate resolutions and demonstrate the employee's willingness to work within the organizational framework. Furthermore, employees should prepare for these conversations by outlining their concerns clearly and proposing potential solutions. This proactive approach not only fosters a positive dialogue but also positions the employee as a constructive participant in the resolution process.

In addition to documenting specific incidents, it is vital to establish a clear record of grievances that outlines the nature of the complaints and the responses received from management. This record should encompass all attempts made to seek resolution, including any meetings held, emails exchanged, and responses provided by management. In Delia's case, the absence of documentation regarding the prescribing doctor's rationale for her medication, as well as the lack of inquiry into her medical history, highlights the need for clarity and transparency in communication. By maintaining a detailed record, employees substantiate their claims and demonstrate that they have made a concerted effort to resolve the issues internally. Moreover, this record serves as a reference point for future discussions with management, ensuring that all parties are on the same page regarding the ongoing issues and the steps taken to address them.

Many organizations have established internal mechanisms for addressing grievances, such as human resources departments or employee assistance programs. Prior to escalating matters to the EEOC, employees should familiarize themselves with these resources and utilize them effectively. In Delia's scenario, if the wellness center had a human resources representative, Geraldine could have sought their assistance in addressing her medication concerns. Engaging with these internal resources not only provides an opportunity for resolution but also demonstrates to the EEOC that the employee has made a genuine effort to resolve the issue before seeking external intervention. Additionally, employees should be aware of any formal grievance procedures outlined in their employee handbook, as following these protocols can further strengthen their case should they need to escalate the matter.

Filing an EEOC complaint is a significant decision that can have profound implications for both the employee and the employer. Once a complaint is filed, the employer is notified, and an investigation ensues. This process can lead to various outcomes, including mediation, determination of reasonable cause, or even litigation. Therefore, employees must weigh the potential consequences of their actions and consider whether all internal avenues for resolution have been thoroughly explored. In Delia's case, understanding the implications of her complaint regarding her medication could have influenced her decision-making process. Employees should also consider the potential impact on their working relationships and the workplace environment, as filing a complaint may lead to tension or retaliation, which could further complicate the situation.

The decision to file an EEOC complaint should not be taken lightly. Employees must exhaust all internal avenues for resolution before proceeding with such a significant action. This involves meticulous documentation of incidents, effective communication with management, and the establishment of a clear record of grievances. By engaging with internal resources and seeking resolution within the organizational framework, employees enhance their chances of a favorable outcome and demonstrate their commitment to resolving issues amicably. Ultimately, the pre-EEOC complaint process serves as a critical step in ensuring that workplace rights are upheld and that employees are afforded the opportunity to address their grievances in a constructive manner. By taking these preliminary steps, employees empower themselves and contribute to a more equitable and respectful workplace environment.

The landscape of prior filings encompasses a variety of documents, each serving a specific purpose. Among the most common types are registration statements, periodic reports, and proxy statements.

This must be addressed immediately. The pattern of behavior exhibited by Melissa Valdez and the management at Gary Job Corps is not only unethical but also illegal. The failure to uphold Human Resources policies and the blatant disregard for employee rights create a toxic work environment that is detrimental to all staff members. It is crucial to recognize that discrimination can manifest in various forms, and it is imperative to hold all individuals accountable, regardless of their race or position within the organization.

The experiences of Geraldine Taylor, including unjust demotions, harassment, and unfounded accusations, highlighted a systemic issue that could not be ignored. Such actions violated workplace policies and infringed upon basic human rights. It was essential for organizations to foster an inclusive and respectful workplace where all employees felt safe and valued.

By bringing these issues to the attention of the Department of Labor, Geraldine's advocate aimed to initiate a thorough investigation into the practices at Gary Job Corps. Accountability and change were necessary. The plea urged the Department to take the complaint seriously and facilitate a meeting to discuss these matters in detail. Together, efforts could ensure no employee would have to endure the mistreatment that Geraldine and others had faced. Enough was enough—it was time for justice and reform in the workplace.

The correspondence addressed to the United States Department of Labor, specifically to Mr. Robert Nowicki, Regional Nurse Consultant, served as a pivotal document encapsulating grievances and concerns regarding the treatment of employees at the Gary Job Corps Center. Dated November 17, 2005, the letter was not merely a reflection of individual discontent but rather a manifestation of systemic issues that had arisen following the transition of management from the Texas Educational Foundation to Management Training Inc. The significance of this communication lies in its potential to illuminate broader implications of management practices on employee welfare, job satisfaction, and the overall efficacy of the Job Corps program. By examining the contents of the letter, critical insights could be gained into the challenges faced by employees and the potential consequences for the students they served.

The Gary Job Corps Center, a vital component of the Job Corps program, historically provided educational and vocational training to young individuals, facilitating their transition into the workforce. Established to empower youth, the center employed numerous professionals, including nurses, who played an essential role in ensuring students' health and well-being. Geraldine Taylor, a dedicated nurse with 28 years of experience within the program, epitomized the commitment many employees had toward the mission of the Job Corps. Her long-standing service underlined the importance of stability and continuity in staffing, crucial for maintaining the quality of care and support provided to the students. The center served as a beacon of hope for at-risk youth, offering education and essential life skills for their future success.

The dedicated staff, including educators, counselors, and healthcare professionals, worked tirelessly to create a nurturing environment fostering personal growth and development. However, recent changes in management raised concerns about the sustainability of this supportive atmosphere. Comparing the management style of the outgoing contractor, Texas Educational Foundation, to that of Management Training Inc., revealed stark contrasts. In the case of *Taylor v. Management Training,* interrogatories explored her employment and treatment under the previous company, leading to an examination of the transition for legal teams to determine her standing before accepting employment with MTC.

Transition of Management and Its Implications

The transition from the Texas Educational Foundation to Management Training Inc. was marked by significant operational changes, which unfortunately led to increased employee turnover. This phenomenon was indicative of deeper issues that warranted examination. The management style adopted by Management Training Inc. lacked support for staff, demonstrated inadequate communication, and failed to recognize the contributions of long-serving employees. Such an environment led to feelings of disenfranchisement among staff, ultimately affecting their performance and the quality of services provided to students.

The implications of this management transition extended beyond employee dissatisfaction. Students, who relied on the center for guidance and support, were also affected. When experienced staff members left, continuity of care was disrupted, and students often found themselves without the mentorship they needed to thrive. This cycle of turnover created an unstable environment, undermining the Job Corps program's mission.

The departure of seasoned staff not only impacted the immediate availability of guidance but also eroded the institutional knowledge crucial for maintaining quality care and education. These experienced individuals brought years of expertise, established relationships with students, and a deep understanding of the program's values and goals. Their absence left a void difficult to fill, resulting in a loss of stability and consistency for students relying on their support.

Frequent turnover also led to a sense of instability among students, making it challenging to build the trust necessary for their development. This environment of constant change diminished students' confidence in the program and their motivation to engage fully in education and training. The ripple effect of turnover extended to remaining employees, who faced increased workloads and stress, leading to burnout and further turnover, perpetuating a cycle that compromised both the program's effectiveness and the well-being of its staff and students.

Addressing this issue required concerted efforts to improve staff retention by fostering a supportive and engaging work environment. Providing opportunities for professional development, recognizing dedication, and ensuring a healthy work-life balance were essential steps to retain experienced staff. By doing so, the Job Corps program could maintain the continuity of care and mentorship vital to students' success.

Employee Grievances and Concerns

The grievances articulated in the letter to Mr. Nowicki were not isolated incidents but rather a culmination of shared experiences among employees at the Gary Job Corps Center. Complaints ranged from inadequate staffing levels compromising care quality to a lack of recognition for the hard work exhibited by long-term employees like Geraldine Taylor. The high turnover rate resulted in a loss of institutional knowledge, critical for the center's effective functioning.

Specific instances of mismanagement exacerbated employee frustrations. Employees reported feeling overwhelmed by understaffing, leading to increased stress and burnout. This situation affected staff morale and compromised the quality of care provided to students, who often did not receive the attention and support they needed to succeed.

The Role of Communication in Employee Relations

Effective communication is the cornerstone of strong employee relations. It plays a pivotal role in creating a positive workplace environment, fostering collaboration, and enhancing overall productivity. Key aspects of how communication impacts employee relations include:

- **Building Trust and Transparency:** Open and honest communication builds trust between management and employees. When employees feel informed and understand the reasoning behind decisions, they are more likely to trust their leaders and feel secure in their roles.
- **Conflict Resolution:** Clear communication channels are essential for resolving conflicts promptly and effectively. When employees feel comfortable voicing their concerns, issues can be addressed before they escalate, promoting a harmonious work environment.
- **Employee Engagement:** Regular and meaningful communication keeps employees engaged and connected to the organization's goals. Providing updates, seeking feedback, and recognizing achievements make employees feel valued and part of the company's success.
- **Performance Management:** Effective communication is crucial for setting clear expectations, providing feedback, and conducting performance reviews. Constructive feedback helps employees understand their strengths and areas for improvement, leading to professional growth.
- **Promoting Inclusivity and Diversity:** Inclusive communication practices ensure all employees feel heard and respected, regardless

of their background. This fosters a culture of diversity and inclusion, where every voice is valued.

- **Change Management:** During times of change, transparent communication helps manage uncertainty and anxiety. Keeping employees informed about changes and the reasons behind them can mitigate resistance and create a more adaptable workforce.

- **Enhancing Team Collaboration:** Open lines of communication encourage collaboration and teamwork. When team members share information and ideas freely, it leads to better problem-solving and innovation.

- **Employee Morale and Satisfaction:** Positive communication contributes to higher employee morale and job satisfaction. When employees feel their input is valued and there is a two-way communication channel, they are more likely to be satisfied with their jobs.

In summary, communication is a vital tool for nurturing strong employee relations. By prioritizing clear, open, and inclusive communication, organizations can create a supportive and engaging work environment where employees thrive.

Communication Challenges at Gary Job Corps Center

Effective communication is a cornerstone of any successful organization, particularly in environments such as the Gary Job Corps Center, where collaboration among staff is essential for delivering comprehensive care to students. The letter to Mr. Nowicki underscores the importance of open communication between management and employees. The previous management under the Texas Educational Foundation was noted for its fairness and transparency—qualities that appear to have diminished under the new management.

This decline in communication exacerbated employee grievances and created an atmosphere of mistrust, hindering the collaborative efforts necessary for the center's success. Furthermore, the lack of communication led to misunderstandings and misalignment of goals between management and staff. When employees felt their concerns were not being heard or addressed, it fostered a sense of alienation and disengagement. This disconnect ultimately resulted in a decline in the quality of services provided to students, as staff members were less motivated to go above and beyond in their roles.

Impact of Management Practices on Morale

The management practices employed by Management Training Inc. profoundly impacted employee morale. The lack of support and recognition for staff contributions led to a decline in job satisfaction, evidenced by increasing turnover rates. Employees who felt undervalued were less likely to invest their full potential into their roles, resulting in diminished quality of care for students. The emotional toll of working in a high-stress environment without adequate support further contributed to burnout, exacerbating staffing issues at the center.

The negative impact on morale created a ripple effect throughout the organization. Unhappy employees contributed to a toxic work environment, affecting individual performance and team dynamics. This hindered collaboration and teamwork—essential elements for providing comprehensive support to students. As a result, the overall effectiveness of the Job Corps program was compromised, ultimately affecting the youth it aimed to serve.

Legal and Ethical Considerations

The concerns raised in the letter to the Department of Labor also involved legal and ethical considerations surrounding employee treatment and workplace conditions. The Job Corps program was designed to provide a supportive environment for both students and staff, and any practices undermining this mission required scrutiny.

The ethical implications of management decisions prioritizing profit over employee welfare were significant, affecting not only the individuals directly involved but also the broader community relying on the services provided by the Job Corps. Moreover, the legal ramifications of poor management practices could not be overlooked. Employees feeling their rights were violated or working in unsafe or unhealthy conditions might seek legal recourse, leading to costly lawsuits and reputational damage for the Job Corps program. These challenges further complicated the already difficult situation at the Gary Job Corps Center.

Considering the issues presented, several recommendations were proposed to enhance the working conditions at the Gary Job Corps Center. Firstly, a thorough review of management practices was suggested to identify areas for improvement. This review included input from employees at all levels to ensure that their voices were heard and considered in the decision-making process. Secondly, implementing regular training and professional development opportunities for staff could foster a sense of growth and investment in their roles. Additionally, establishing a formal recognition program to celebrate employee achievements was seen as a significant way to boost morale and encourage retention.

Furthermore, enhancing communication channels between management and staff was deemed crucial. Regular meetings, feedback sessions, and anonymous surveys provided employees with a platform to voice their concerns and suggestions. By fostering a culture of open communication, management could rebuild trust and create a more collaborative work environment.

Lastly, prioritizing employee well-being through initiatives such as mental health support and stress management programs was identified as a way to mitigate burnout and improve overall job satisfaction.

The letter addressed to Mr. Robert Nowicki of the US Department of Labor, an overseer of Job Corps, served as a critical reflection of the challenges faced by employees at the Gary Job Corps Center following the transition to new management. The concerns articulated within this correspondence highlighted the need for a reevaluation of management practices to ensure they aligned with the foundational mission of the Job Corps program. By addressing the grievances of employees and fostering a supportive work environment, it became possible to enhance both employee satisfaction and the quality of services provided to students. Ultimately, the implications of this discussion extended beyond the confines of the Gary Job Corps Center; they resonated with broader themes of employee welfare, organizational ethics, and the imperative for effective management in educational settings. The future success of the Job Corps program hinged on the ability of its management to recognize and address these critical issues, ensuring that both employees and students could thrive in a supportive and empowering environment.

In the realm of legal representation, the efficacy and commitment of an attorney significantly influenced the outcomes of a case. This discussion sought to explore the implications of poor legal representation, particularly through the lens of Chris Pittard's handling of a case involving adverse employment actions. The discussion delved into the nuances of legal representation, the historical context of employment discrimination laws, and the ramifications of inadequate legal support in the pursuit of justice. By examining these elements, it was possible to better understand the critical importance of effective legal advocacy in ensuring fair treatment within the workplace.

Introduction to Legal Representation

Legal representation was a cornerstone of the judicial process, serving as the bridge between the complexities of the law and the individuals seeking justice. An attorney's role extended beyond mere advocacy; it encompassed the responsibility to provide informed guidance, emotional support, and strategic insights throughout the legal proceedings. In the case of Chris Pattard, the perceived lack of aggression and support during the early stages of the case raised critical questions about the standards of legal representation and the expectations clients held for their attorneys. The attorney-client relationship was foundational, and when it faltered, the consequences were dire for those seeking justice.

The Role of an Attorney in Employment Discrimination Cases

Employment discrimination cases, particularly those involving adverse employment actions, required a nuanced understanding of both legal principles and the specific circumstances surrounding the case. Adverse employment actions included termination, demotion, or other significant changes in employment status that were detrimental to the employee. An attorney's ability to navigate these complexities was vital, as the legal landscape was often fraught with intricate regulations and precedents that had to be meticulously analyzed and applied. Furthermore, attorneys needed to be adept at gathering evidence, interviewing witnesses, and constructing compelling arguments that resonated with judges and juries alike. This multifaceted role demanded not only legal acumen but also a deep understanding of the emotional and psychological toll that discrimination took on individuals.

Clients often entered the legal system with a myriad of questions and concerns, seeking clarity and direction. However, when attorneys failed to provide timely answers or exhibited a lack of proactive engagement, clients felt abandoned and disillusioned. In the case at hand, the absence of sufficient communication from Chris Pattard not only hindered the progression of the case but also contributed to a sense of uncertainty and frustration among the clients. This situation underscored the importance of establishing a robust attorney-client relationship characterized by transparency, trust, and mutual respect. Clients needed to feel empowered to voice their concerns and expectations, and attorneys had to be willing to listen and adapt their strategies accordingly.

To fully comprehend the implications of adverse employment actions and the legal frameworks governing them, it was essential to examine the historical context of employment discrimination laws in the United States. The foundation of these laws could be traced back to significant legislative milestones, including the Civil Rights Act of 1964 and subsequent executive orders aimed at promoting equal employment opportunities. These laws were born out of a necessity to combat systemic inequalities and ensure that all individuals, regardless of race, gender, or other characteristics, had the right to fair treatment in the workplace. Understanding this historical backdrop was crucial for both attorneys and clients as they navigated the complexities of employment discrimination cases.

CHAPTER TEN: A PIVOTAL MOMENT IN EMPLOYMENT LAW

Executive Order 10925, signed by President John F. Kennedy in March 1961, marked a significant turning point in the fight against employment discrimination. This order prohibited federal government contractors from discriminating based on race and established the President's Committee on Equal Employment Opportunity. The implications of this order were profound, as it not only set a precedent for future legislation but also underscored the federal government's commitment to addressing systemic discrimination in the workplace. The establishment of this committee was a crucial step in ensuring that complaints of discrimination were taken seriously and addressed in a timely manner, thereby laying the groundwork for more comprehensive anti-discrimination laws in the years to come.

Executive Order 10925: Shaping Legal Representation

The enactment of Executive Order 10925 necessitated a shift in the legal landscape, compelling attorneys to adapt their strategies and approaches to align with the evolving standards of employment law. In this context, the role of an attorney became increasingly critical, as they were tasked with interpreting and applying these new regulations to protect the rights of their clients. However, as evidenced by the experiences of clients represented by Chris Pattard, the effectiveness of legal representation varied significantly, leading to disparities in the pursuit of justice. Attorneys needed not only to be knowledgeable about the law but also to be proactive in advocating for their clients' rights, ensuring that they were both heard and understood within the legal framework.

The ramifications of poor legal representation extended beyond the immediate outcomes of a case; they had lasting effects on the lives of clients. When attorneys failed to advocate vigorously for their clients, the likelihood of achieving a favorable resolution diminished. Furthermore, clients often experienced emotional distress and a sense of powerlessness, exacerbating the challenges they faced in navigating the legal system. In cases of adverse employment actions, the stakes were particularly high, as individuals found themselves fighting not only for their jobs but also for their dignity and livelihoods.

The psychological impact of inadequate representation could lead to long-term consequences, such as diminished self-esteem and increased anxiety, which further complicated the healing process after experiencing discrimination. For many, their job was more than just a means of earning a living; it represented a significant part of their identity and self-worth. When faced with unfair treatment or discrimination, the emotional toll was profound. Feeling unsupported or misrepresented in these situations only exacerbated stress and anxiety, making it harder for individuals to recover and move forward. The effects of such experiences rippled through every aspect of a person's life, affecting their mental health, personal relationships, and overall well-being.

It was crucial for organizations to recognize the importance of providing robust support and fair representation to their employees. Ensuring that employees felt heard, valued, and protected could make a significant difference in their ability to cope with and overcome challenges in the workplace. Ultimately, fostering a supportive and inclusive environment not only benefited the individuals involved but also strengthened the entire organization, leading to a more positive, productive, and harmonious workplace.

Mitigating Challenges in Legal Representation

To mitigate the challenges associated with inadequate legal representation, several strategies were proposed. First and foremost, fostering open lines of communication between attorneys and clients was essential. Regular updates and transparent discussions about case developments helped alleviate client concerns and built trust. Additionally, attorneys were encouraged to prioritize ongoing education and training to stay abreast of changes in employment law and best practices for representation. This commitment to professional development not only enhanced the attorney's skill set but also ensured that clients received the most informed and effective advocacy possible.

Client Empowerment: Unlocking Potential

Empowering clients to take an active role in their legal proceedings enhanced the overall effectiveness of legal representation. By encouraging clients to ask questions, seek clarification, and engage in the decision-making process, attorneys fostered a collaborative environment that promoted a sense of agency and involvement. This approach not only strengthened the attorney-client relationship but also equipped clients with the knowledge and confidence necessary to navigate the complexities of their cases. When clients felt empowered, they were more likely to remain engaged and proactive, which often led to better outcomes in their legal battles.

The Fallout of Inadequate Legal Advocacy

The case of Chris Pattard, the representing attorney of the first EEOC case for Taylor and Steen, served as a poignant reminder of the critical role that effective legal representation played in the pursuit of justice, particularly in the context of employment discrimination. The historical evolution of employment laws, exemplified by Executive

Order 10925, elevated the role of dedicated and informed legal advocates. As the legal landscape continued to evolve, it was imperative that both attorneys and clients worked collaboratively to ensure that the principles of justice and equality were upheld. Ultimately, the pursuit of justice was a shared responsibility, and the quality of legal representation significantly influenced the outcomes of individuals seeking redress for adverse employment actions.

Pattard failed to meet the obligations to represent his clients effectively. The experience of receiving a letter from the attorney, which informed them of the court's dismissal of their case due to Summary Judgment, marked a profoundly disheartening moment in their legal journey. The initial confusion they encountered compelled them to meticulously re-read the correspondence multiple times, ultimately leading them to seek clarification from Pattard. Unfortunately, his communication regarding the court's decision lacked the necessary comfort and clarity. When asked about the next steps, his response was disconcerting: *"I will be moving to a new law firm, and I don't think they will want to follow through with this type of case."*

This statement not only left the clients in a state of uncertainty but also raised significant questions about the commitment and resources available to them in pursuing their legal rights. Their desire to understand the rationale behind the court's judgment in favor of MTC/Gary was met with insufficient explanation from Pattard, who merely indicated that the opposing counsel had presented a more compelling case to the court. Upon reviewing the documentation, they discovered that the opposing firm had cited approximately fifty different cases, many of which bore no relevance to their situation. These cases, while establishing precedents in other contexts, were not adequately challenged by Pattard, who appeared to lack the necessary resources to conduct thorough research and effectively contest the filings presented against them.

Subsequently, Pattard was instructed to return all case files so that alternative legal representation could be sought to re-file the case. However, it became increasingly apparent that he was dissuading his clients from pursuing this course of action. During this tumultuous period, Geraldine, Glenda, and their colleagues recognized a troubling dynamic: during the deposition in Austin, Texas, Pattard exhibited a notably friendly rapport with Melissa Valdez, the human resources manager for Gary. His prior admission of seeking employment with another law firm further complicated the trust in his commitment to the case.

Observing Pattard's demeanor during the deposition, particularly after receiving a job offer, raised concerns about his dedication to advocating for his clients' interests. His lack of initiative in calling witnesses to testify underscored the inadequacies of the legal representation, ultimately contributing to the pervasive sense of poor legal advocacy. The experience of receiving a letter from the attorney regarding the dismissal of the case to Summary Judgment stood as one of the most bewildering and distressing moments in their lives.

The initial shock of the notification was compounded by a profound sense of confusion, leading them to re-read the letter multiple times to grasp the implications of the court's decision. In their quest for clarity, they reached out to Pattard, whose response did little to alleviate their concerns. His communication lacked comfort and reassurance, leaving them with more questions than answers. Upon inquiring about the next steps following the dismissal, Pattard's reply was disheartening: *"I will be moving to a new law firm, and I don't think they will want to follow through with this type of case."*

This revelation not only added to their anxiety but also raised critical questions about the future of their legal battle. They were left grappling with the reality that their case had been dismissed in favor of MTC/Gary, yet the rationale behind this judgment remained elusive.

In discussions with Pattard, it became evident that he was unable to provide a comprehensive explanation of the judicial process that led to the unfavorable outcome. He merely indicated that the opposing counsel had presented a significantly more compelling case to the court. This assertion prompted the clients to conduct their own review of the documentation associated with the case. To their dismay, they discovered that the opposing firm had cited approximately fifty different cases, many of which appeared irrelevant to their situation.

This extensive citation not only demonstrated the opposing counsel's legal acumen but also highlighted a critical deficiency in their own representation. The opposing counsel's strategic approach and thorough preparation played a significant role in influencing the court's decision. Their ability to present such a vast array of cases, even if tangentially related, showcased their legal prowess and understanding of the judicial system's nuances. In stark contrast, the representation provided by Pattard seemed lacking in both depth and strategic insight, which undoubtedly contributed to the unfavorable outcome.

The implications of this were profound. Not only did it underscore the importance of having a well-prepared and knowledgeable legal team, but it also highlighted the need for thorough and meticulous case preparation. Faith in Pattard's ability to represent the case effectively was severely shaken, prompting a reconsideration of the legal strategy moving forward. It raised the question of whether he had given the case the attention and rigor it deserved, and if his lack of comprehensive explanation reflected deeper issues in his approach.

Moving forward, it became imperative to address these deficiencies. Securing a legal representative fully equipped to handle the complexities of the case with the diligence and expertise required was essential. This included understanding and applying relevant precedents and anticipating and countering the strategies employed by opposing counsel. The experience with Pattard served as a cautionary tale of the critical importance of thorough preparation and strategic planning in the legal arena.

Ultimately, the situation underscored the vital need for accountability and excellence in legal representation. As the team navigated the complexities of their legal challenges, they became more determined than ever to secure the competent and proactive advocacy necessary to achieve a just outcome. The cited cases, while setting precedents in various legal contexts, underscored the challenges they faced in contesting the dismissal. Pattard's admission of lacking the resources necessary to thoroughly research and challenge the opposing filings was particularly troubling. It became increasingly clear that the legal representation was not equipped to navigate the complexities of the case, which ultimately contributed to the unfavorable judgment.

This realization profoundly impacted their understanding of the legal system and the importance of competent legal representation. The dismissal of the case to Summary Judgment was not merely a procedural setback; it represented a significant personal and emotional challenge. The confusion and frustration experienced were exacerbated by the lack of clear communication from the attorney, which ultimately left them feeling abandoned in a critical moment of need.

Reflecting on this ordeal, it became evident that the complexities of legal proceedings demanded not only a thorough understanding of the law but also a commitment to effective communication and advocacy on behalf of clients. The legal system, intricate and intimidating, made the role of an attorney crucial—not just in terms of legal acumen, but also in providing clear guidance and support to their clients.

This journey underscored the necessity of having a legal representative who was not only knowledgeable and experienced but also compassionate and communicative. The experience highlighted the critical need for transparency and regular updates from legal counsel.

Moving forward, they resolved to be more vigilant in selecting legal representation. Traits such as empathy, responsiveness, and a proactive approach to client communication became paramount. It is their hope that by sharing this story, others could navigate their own legal challenges with greater awareness and confidence.

Conclusion

The dismissal of the case to Summary Judgment served as a poignant reminder of the vulnerabilities inherent in the legal process. The experience illuminated the necessity for diligent legal representation and the critical role that effective communication played in navigating complex legal landscapes.

As the timeline to appeal or file a new case loomed, the struggles to secure new representation were compounded by urgency. The case of *Dark Hearts Iron Hands,* after the Summary Judgment rendered in the United States Court for the Western District of Texas, proceeded to appeal in the 5th Circuit Court of the United States. This next phase required justification and explanation of factors previously excluded as evidence, offering a renewed opportunity to seek remedy from a higher court.

CHAPTER ELEVEN: GERALDINE'S LEGAL SPOTLIGHT

Geraldine's position as a medical technician exemplifies the intersection of healthcare and social rehabilitation, where providing medical care intricately connects to the emotional and psychological support individuals require in their journey toward recovery. In an environment characterized by uncertainty and potential turmoil, her unwavering dedication serves as a stabilizing force, fostering a sense of security among the students. This duality of care — both physical and emotional — underscores the necessity of a holistic approach to health, where the psychological well-being of individuals is prioritized alongside their medical needs.

Furthermore, Geraldine's interactions with the students often extend beyond clinical assessments; they include moments of empathy and understanding, reinforcing the notion that healthcare professionals play a pivotal role in shaping the lived experiences of those they serve.

The narrator's apprehension regarding Geraldine's safety poignantly reflects broader societal concerns about the well-being of healthcare staff in high-stress environments. The inherent risks associated with working in such settings often blur the lines between care and danger, creating a complex dynamic where professionals must navigate their responsibilities while safeguarding their own well-being. This tension is particularly pronounced in contexts where the potential for violence or emotional distress is ever-present, necessitating a robust support system for healthcare providers. The narrative captures this struggle, illustrating how the fear for Geraldine's safety resonates not only with the narrator but also with the community at large, emphasizing the urgent need for systemic changes that prioritize the protection and support of healthcare workers.

As the narrative unfolds, it becomes increasingly evident that the struggles faced by the narrator — balancing the demands of marriage, education, and financial instability — reflect the broader challenges many individuals encounter in their pursuit of aspirations. These personal struggles enrich the narrative, humanizing the experience of those involved in the healthcare system. The complexities of navigating personal and professional responsibilities underscore the multifaceted nature of life in high-stress environments, where the pursuit of one's goals is often fraught with obstacles. Moreover, the narrator's journey resonates universally, encapsulating the trials and tribulations that many face in their quest for stability and fulfillment.

Geraldine serves as a powerful representation of the intersection between healthcare and social rehabilitation, highlighting the critical role that dedicated professionals play in the lives of those they serve. Her presence in the infirmary not only provides essential medical care but also fosters a sense of hope and security among the students. The apprehension felt by the narrator regarding Geraldine's safety underscores the broader societal concerns surrounding the well-being of healthcare providers in high-stress environments, emphasizing the urgent need for systemic changes that prioritize their protection. Furthermore, the narrator's personal struggles enrich the narrative, reflecting the universal challenges encountered in the pursuit of aspirations. Ultimately, this exploration of Geraldine's role and the surrounding dynamics illuminates the profound impact of healthcare professionals on individual lives and the necessity of supporting those who dedicate themselves to such vital work.

The Gary Job Corps Center, established in 1964, serves as a poignant case study in the dynamics of violence and social stratification within educational institutions. The environment, characterized by palpable tension among students, often necessitated a defensive posture among staff members, who were frequently left to navigate the complexities of a volatile atmosphere. The targeting of white students by their black counterparts, driven by racial animosities or regional affiliations, exemplifies the deeply entrenched divisions permeating the center. This pervasive fear among certain student demographics led to a significant attrition rate, as individuals chose to withdraw from the program rather than confront the potential for violence.

Moreover, the reluctance of Asian students to engage in communal activities further underscores the isolating effects of such an environment, where the instinct for self-preservation often supersedes the desire for academic achievement. This phenomenon can be attributed to various factors, including cultural expectations and the pervasive pressure to excel academically, which may inadvertently foster a sense of alienation among peers. Furthermore, the spectrum of violence observed — ranging from physical altercations to more grievous acts involving weapons — paints a stark picture of the challenges faced by both students and staff. The harrowing incidents, including stabbings and the tragic murder of a young girl, not only prompted federal investigations but also highlighted the precarious nature of safety within the confines of what was ostensibly an educational facility.

Consequently, the implications of such violence extend beyond immediate physical harm; they permeate the psychological well-being of the student body, engendering an atmosphere of fear and mistrust that can stifle academic engagement and communal interaction. In addition, the systemic issues contributing to this environment warrant comprehensive examination, as they reveal the intricate interplay between societal pressures and individual responses to adversity.

CHAPTER TWELVE: UNDERSTANDING OF THE INSTITUTIONAL CULTURE

The role of Geraldine, who frequently transported injured students to the medical facility, illustrates the inherent risks faced by staff members. The anxiety surrounding her safety, coupled with the unpredictable behavior of students, reflects a broader concern regarding the adequacy of protective measures for those tasked with maintaining order. Over time, a deeper understanding of the institutional culture emerged, revealing a staff dynamic that was equally fraught with territoriality and resistance to new personnel. This complex interplay of fear, respect, and survival within the Job Corps Center encapsulates the profound challenges inherent in fostering a safe and conducive learning environment amidst the shadows of violence and division.

The center was in dire need of extensive repairs, and the paramount concern was the safety and well-being of the students. In this context, a significant question arose regarding the potential implications of placing students on leave status; specifically, it became crucial to ascertain how many would ultimately return to the center to fulfill their academic commitments. This inquiry not only highlights the precarious nature of the situation but also underscores the necessity for a strategic approach to ensure that students feel supported and motivated to re-engage with their educational environment. Consequently, the administration must consider implementing measures that facilitate a smooth transition back to the center, fostering a sense of community and continuity amidst the challenges posed by the current circumstances.

In examining Geraldine's multifaceted character and her professional trajectory, it becomes evident that her ability to compartmentalize her emotions not only served as a coping mechanism but also as a catalyst for her personal and professional growth. *This nuanced approach to her responsibilities allowed her to navigate the complexities of her dual roles with remarkable efficacy.* Furthermore, the ritualistic sharing of daily experiences with her family not only provided a therapeutic outlet but also reinforced the significance of familial solidarity in the face of external adversities.

Geraldine's even-mindedness, characterized by her quiet yet perceptive nature, reflects a profound understanding of the dynamics within her work environment. By consciously choosing to remain uninvolved in the personal affairs of her colleagues, she adeptly maintained her reputation as a diligent and principled worker, which, in turn, fortified her standing within both her professional and domestic spheres. Despite the systemic challenges she faced, including being consistently overlooked and underpaid, her unwavering commitment to the Job Corps program exemplifies a significant dedication to her vocation.

The transformative journey that Geraldine undertook over the course of five years is emblematic of resilience and the pursuit of excellence. As she evolved into a master of her craft as a medical technician, her ascent to leadership roles — such as wellness center shift leader and center pregnancy coordinator — underscores her capacity for growth and adaptation. This trajectory not only highlights her professional achievements but also serves as a testament to the profound impact of perseverance in overcoming institutional barriers. Consequently, Geraldine's story resonates as an inspiring narrative of empowerment, illustrating how individual agency can flourish amidst systemic challenges.

In summary, the early life of Geraldine Williams is a testament to the profound impact of familial and communal influences on individual development. Her journey from the small town of Chappell Hill to the broader world is marked by a continuous thread of service, resilience, and faith. As she navigated the complexities of her upbringing, Geraldine emerged as a figure embodying the values of her community, driven by a desire to make a significant difference in the lives of others. This narrative not only highlights the significance of her early experiences but also serves as a reflection on the enduring power of family and community in shaping one's identity and aspirations.

In the beginning, the narrative unfolds within the intricate tapestry of *Dark Hears Iron Hands,* subtitled *The Conspiracies,* which serves as a profound exploration of the multifaceted nature of human existence and the underlying forces that shape reality. This work delves into the realms of analytic philosophy and metaphysics, inviting readers to engage with the complex interplay between perception and reality, as well as the epistemological inquiries that arise from such interactions.

The title itself evokes a sense of foreboding and intrigue, suggesting that the characters are ensnared in a web of conspiratorial machinations that challenge their autonomy and moral agency. As the plot progresses, the narrative intricately weaves together various philosophical themes, including transcendental idealism and the categorical imperative, compelling the audience to reflect on the ethical implications of their choices and the nature of truth in a world rife with deception.

Furthermore, the author employs a nuanced approach to character development, allowing for a profound examination of the motivations and desires that drive individuals toward both altruistic and malevolent actions. This duality not only enriches the narrative but also serves as a vehicle for broader philosophical discourse, prompting readers to synthesize their understanding of morality within the context of the unfolding conspiracies.

To sum up, *Dark Hears Iron Hands: The Conspiracies* is a significant addition to contemporary literature, offering a diverse array of ideas that resonate with the complexity of human experience. The exploration of these themes not only enhances the narrative depth but also invites critical reflection on the nature of existence itself, thereby establishing a compelling foundation for further inquiry into the philosophical dimensions of the text.

The narrative begins against a backdrop of uncertainty and ambition, encapsulating the profound challenges faced by a newly married couple navigating the complexities of life in a small town. The initial depiction of darkness, where "shameful behaviors" lurk, serves as a metaphorical representation of the societal obstacles that often impede progress, particularly for those striving for higher education and meaningful employment. Aspirations are contrasted with what seems to be a stagnant environment, highlighting the couple's determination to transcend their circumstances.

As their journey begins, the couple's decision to move to San Marcos, Texas, symbolizes a desire for independence and personal growth. The description of the town as "primitive in nature" underscores the challenges inherent in their pursuit of growth, both personally and professionally. Individuals often struggle with the conflict between ambition and the limitations imposed by their surroundings, as they strive for a "good job and a decent place to live," which becomes a metaphor for the larger human experience.

The story also introduces the couple's professional aspirations, with Geraldine's employment at the Sweetbriar nursing home playing a key role. This setting facilitates the rekindling of their relationship while illustrating the interconnectedness of personal and professional lives. The reference to the author's return to the Brenham area after military service adds complexity, reflecting the transition from a structured environment to the uncertainties of civilian life, all while pursuing a degree in law enforcement at Blinn Junior College.

This narrative spans a significant period of transformation, distinguished by resilience and the quest for knowledge in the face of adversity. By examining the couple's experiences, readers can reflect on personal growth and community development, using their journey as a microcosm of broader societal dynamics.

During Geraldine's early employment, Arthur found himself in a precarious position, as he had not yet secured a role within the organization. His concerns for Geraldine's safety, following a disconcerting encounter with several students, loomed large. Arthur began to notice that his chances of employment were diminishing as he waited for a call regarding his application to the center.

Arthur waited for three weeks before calling to inquire about his application status and was informed to attend an interview. He realized that, even though he had applied for a job in the security department, he was instead offered a position as a dorm attendant in residential living.

Arthur's academic pursuits were rooted in law enforcement and criminal justice, making this unexpected turn of events distant from his aspirations. *Despite adversity, there are times when one must accept available opportunities to fulfill financial obligations and support one's family.* Although the salary of $525 per month was small, it represented a significant financial advancement for Arthur. Even though it wasn't much, it was a step forward. On his first day of training, he encountered a counselor who displayed rude behavior due to his tardiness—an unavoidable consequence of his unfamiliarity with the center's layout. Fortunately, other staff members intervened, defending Arthur and diffusing the situation, providing some support in an otherwise challenging atmosphere.

A vigilant approach to maintaining safety and order among the diverse student body was necessary within the Gary Job Corps Center, established in 1964 and surrounded by tension and conflict. The dynamics of race and regional identity played a significant role in shaping the experiences of students, with white students often targeted by their black counterparts. This created an atmosphere of fear that compelled many to withdraw from the program entirely, underscoring the significant impact of racial tensions and the broader implications for the center's mission to provide a safe haven for all students.

The pervasive atmosphere of violence, characterized by physical altercations and the use of weapons, further complicated the educational landscape. Incidents of stabbings, drug trafficking, and even murder—such as the tragic case of a young girl found deceased under a pile of lumber—necessitated intervention from federal authorities. The involvement of the FBI underscored the severity of the situation while illustrating the complexities of managing a federally funded institution where students were classified as federal employees, while staff operated under a different set of regulations.

Moreover, the role of staff members, particularly in their interactions with students, revealed a microcosm of territoriality and resistance to change. New employees often faced significant challenges in gaining the respect and trust of their more established colleagues, hindering their ability to address the behavioral issues prevalent among the student population. This intricate web of relationships and power dynamics within the center influenced daily operations and had lasting implications for the program's overall efficacy in achieving its educational objectives.

In summary, the experiences at the Gary Job Corps Center during this tumultuous period serve as a poignant reminder of the complexities inherent in educational environments characterized by diversity and conflict. The interplay of fear, violence, and institutional dynamics shaped the individual experiences of students and staff alike, raising critical questions about the efficacy of such programs in fostering a safe and supportive learning environment.

CHAPTER THIRTEEN: PROFESSIONAL JOURNEY

Arthur vividly remembers the day he was promoted to residential advisor, a moment that marked a watershed in his professional life. After months of tireless dedication, this promotion came with not just increased responsibility but also the power to effect real change. His tenure as a residential advisor became a turning point, transforming the student community before his eyes. Discipline, once sporadic, began to flourish under his watchful presence. Students, aware of his unwavering commitment, began to alter their behaviors, uniting to tackle grave issues like substance abuse, theft, and inter-residential crime.

A landmark initiative during his leadership was the daily skills training session instituted at three o'clock every weekday. This program became a mandatory fixture in the students' lives, teaching them crucial life skills that extended far beyond the classroom. From community living and race relations to employment readiness and leadership development, these sessions became the cornerstone of their routine. A standout lesson, embodied in the simple yet profound mantra *"I'm okay, you're okay,"* wove itself into the fabric of their daily interactions, fostering a sense of mutual respect and understanding that resonated across students, staff, teachers, and the entire community. Arthur's legacy was not just in the policies he implemented but in the palpable shift he orchestrated within the hearts and minds of the students he mentored.

Upon his promotion to senior residential advisor, his performance evaluations soared to unprecedented heights, showcasing his unwavering commitment to excellence. This new role not only affirmed his dedication but also came with the weighty responsibility of acting as a campus supervisor during the frequent absences of regular supervisors — a task that quickly became a hallmark of his duties. Management's increasing trust in him as a reliable and effective leader significantly bolstered his reputation.

In this capacity, Arthur oversaw nine dormitories, housing up to 120 students at any given time, and managed a team of up to 11 staff members during critical shifts that stretched from two-thirty in the afternoon until midnight. This role, despite being the most extensive among the four campuses, was also the most formidable challenge that any residential advisor or campus supervisor could face.

The campus manager, the late Joe Garcia, epitomized strict accountability, enforcing a no-nonsense approach to management. Don Edwards, the campus supervisor, upheld equally high standards of professionalism and discipline, underscoring the importance of a structured and responsible residential environment.

At the onset, the juxtaposition of the most troubled students reaching out to assist others, regardless of past grievances or racial differences, stood as a powerful testament to the resilience of the human spirit. Amidst adversity, a singular focus on mutual care and support emerged as a beacon of hope, lighting the path toward redemption under the most challenging circumstances. The San Marcos Municipal Airport, immortalized in a photograph by Arthur Taylor, silently witnessed this transformative journey.

The staff at Gary, predominantly composed of individuals with military backgrounds, utilized their extensive training to instill discipline and foster accountability among the students. Initially, the security presence at Gary was primarily maintained by Gary personnel, but the involvement of reserve deputies and, ultimately, federal police underscored the escalating need for structured oversight to maintain safety within the center. At one point, the presence of federal marshals alongside uniformed security personnel highlighted the gravity of the situation as the community grappled with the implications of the students' actions.

Despite the palpable animosity directed toward Gary students by the citizens of San Marcos, it is noteworthy that their economic contributions through community service were simultaneously acknowledged and appreciated. This paradox of being both reviled and valued illustrates the complex dynamics at play, as local businesses benefitted from the labor provided by the students, even as they faced restrictions and social ostracism due to past misconduct, including theft and vandalism.

Efforts to monitor student behavior were often thwarted by the inherent challenges of managing a population that, once released from their designated drop-off points, dispersed throughout the community. This reality not only placed additional burdens on local law enforcement but also highlighted the necessity for a more effective system of oversight and support.

Gary's Journey: Efforts to Restore Reputation and Respect

The evolution of Gary was marked by numerous attempts to enhance the center's reputation and restore a semblance of respect among residents. Arthur's assignment to work specifically with students adjudicated as criminally inclined presented both challenges and opportunities. Under his supervision, the potential for rehabilitation and positive change became increasingly apparent, as evidenced by notable improvements in graduation rates and a marked decrease in violent incidents. This experience ultimately reinforced the notion that, even in the most challenging environments, the capacity for growth and transformation remains a significant possibility.

Advancing forward in the context of his promotion to center supervisor, it is imperative to acknowledge the intricate dynamics at play within the organizational structure, particularly the interplay of political maneuvering and personal ambition that ultimately influenced his tenure. *What ostensibly represented a culmination of my dedication and service was overshadowed by the machinations of upper management, who sought to undermine my position.* This situation exemplifies how personal agendas can infiltrate professional environments, leading to a climate of distrust and hostility.

Furthermore, the recommendation from Congressman Bill Patman, while a testament to Arthur's capabilities and contributions, inadvertently positioned him as a target for those who perceived his connections as a threat to their own aspirations. The subsequent pressure to resign, framed as a protective measure against potential political corruption, underscores the extent to which his efforts to unionize the staff were met with resistance. This initiative, aimed at empowering employees and enhancing their working conditions, was viewed not merely as a labor rights movement but as a direct challenge to the established order within the institution.

Consequently, the culmination of these events serves as a poignant reminder of the complexities inherent in organizational politics, where the pursuit of autonomy and advocacy for collective rights can lead to significant repercussions. This experience not only highlights the necessity for vigilance in navigating such environments but also raises critical questions about the ethical implications of leadership and the responsibilities that accompany positions of authority.

The overwhelming number of complaints necessitated the intervention of the local NAACP president. A personal conversation with the Department of Labor representative for the Texas Job Corps Region revealed that these grievances ultimately led to the consideration and subsequent termination of the labor contract with the Department of Labor for the Texas Educational Foundation Inc. in the operation of the local Job Corps center. This marked a significant turning point, as the troubled contractor, which had operated the Gary Job Corps from 1964 to 2000, was on the verge of becoming a relic of the past. The termination of this contract ushered in a dramatic transformation within the Gary Job Corps program, as the opportunity to negotiate the center's operations was opened to other companies nationwide that met the stringent government requirements.

As a result, the center transitioned from the Texas Educational Foundation's management to the Management and Training Corporation based in Utah, shifting from a nonprofit to a profit-driven operational model. This leadership change prompted a wave of notifications to all staff about impending management alterations, igniting a renewed sense of unrest throughout the center. Initially, many employees were excited about the prospect of change, seeing it as a potential remedy for what had become, in the eyes of many, a dysfunctional operation. The atmosphere was charged with newfound motivation, a sentiment notably absent in previous years, as staff members hoped the new employer would foster an environment conducive to advancement and improved income opportunities.

However, this initial enthusiasm soon gave way to apprehension as the staff grappled with the uncertainty of job security amidst significant policy and procedural changes. The prospect of losing their positions, coupled with the potential upheaval of established status within the organization, instilled a sense of fear among the employees. For many, the departure of the Texas Educational Foundation was a welcome development, yet the looming changes brought a complex interplay of hope and anxiety regarding the future of the Job Corps center and its personnel.

At first, the arrival of the management team from MTC heralded a significant shift in the center's operational dynamics, characterized by an ostentatious display of resources and a palpable sense of authority. The introduction of higher-grade government vehicles was perceived by the staff as a harbinger of positive change, fostering an atmosphere of optimism and expectation.

Colleagues remarked, *"These people have it together. If you need something, just ask, and they get it,"* reflecting a belief that the new management would enhance the program's overall efficacy through their willingness to invest in quality. However, this initial impression soon gave way to a more complex reality. It became evident that MTC intended to replace the existing management with their own team, many of whom possessed dubious backgrounds and questionable qualifications. The abrupt dismissal of long-serving staff members, who had cultivated extensive institutional knowledge and demonstrated a capacity for self-sufficiency, raised significant concerns regarding the center's operational sustainability.

The decision to terminate these employees, ostensibly for reasons of efficiency, overlooked the profound expertise and commitment they had contributed over the years. This transition underscored the fragility of institutional memory and the precariousness of change driven solely by economic considerations, leaving many to question the future stability of the Gary Job Corps Center.

Furthermore, the imposition of untrained personnel from other cities only exacerbated the situation. These individuals, thrust into roles for which they had no prior experience or understanding, disrupted not only the educational programs but also jeopardized the quality of medical care provided to the students. The stark disconnect between management's expectations and the reality of the center's services became glaringly apparent when they finally toured the extensive medical facilities. This tour revealed just how out of touch they were with the actual needs and operations of the center, highlighting a profound misalignment that threatened the very foundation of the institution.

Consequently, the initial promise of improved management developed into a scenario marked by inefficiency and disarray, prompting a critical examination of the implications of such top-down interventions in institutional settings. The heavy-handed tactics employed by MTC, juxtaposed against a well-established operational framework, underscore the complexities inherent in organizational change — particularly when it disregards the invaluable contributions of seasoned staff members.

The shift in management styles between the Texas Educational Foundation (TEF) and the current regime highlights a significant transformation in organizational culture. Under TEF, a semblance of stability and accountability was maintained, fostering an environment where employees could anticipate the consequences of their actions and decisions. In stark contrast, the emergence of a management structure characterized by intimidation and arbitrary rule changes has engendered a climate of fear and uncertainty.

The phrase, *"Catch the vision or catch the bus,"* epitomizes the coercive tactics used to enforce compliance while simultaneously alienating those who might otherwise contribute to a more equitable workplace. Furthermore, the insidious nature of the *"good-ole-boy"* system perpetuates a cycle of favoritism and exclusion, wherein opportunities are systematically denied to those who do not conform to the prevailing power dynamics. This reality not only undermines the morale of the workforce but also stifles the potential for diverse perspectives to enrich organizational discourse.

The experiences shared by employees at Gary Job Corps highlight an urgent need for introspection and reform. The quest for a just and inclusive workplace remains an ongoing challenge that demands collective action and sustained commitment.

Within the Gary Job Corps Center, established in 1964, palpable tension often escalated into violence, revealing the complex interplay of race, fear, and survival among the student body. White students were frequently targeted by their black counterparts, ostensibly due to racial prejudices or regional affiliations, underscoring a significant sociocultural divide that permeated the center. This atmosphere of intimidation compelled some students to withdraw from the program entirely, driven by an overwhelming fear for their safety, and highlighted the broader implications of racial dynamics within educational institutions.

Moreover, the reluctance of Asian students to engage in communal activities further illustrated the pervasive climate of fear that stifled collaboration and hindered academic progress. The resort to violence, whether through physical altercations or the use of weapons, reflected a desperate struggle for power and control within a society fraught with conflict.

The harrowing incidents of stabbings, drug trafficking, and even murder, such as the tragic case of a young girl found deceased under construction materials, necessitated federal intervention by the FBI, serving as a grim reminder of the stakes involved in such a volatile environment.

The role of staff members, particularly in their interactions with students, further complicated this narrative. The territorial nature of the staff, coupled with their initial resistance to new employees, created an insular culture that often left newcomers feeling alienated and unsupported. This dynamic, combined with the inherent dangers posed by the student population — particularly in light of Geraldine's role in transporting injured students — accentuated the precariousness of the situation. The fear that permeated the center was not solely confined to the students; it extended to the staff, who were equally vulnerable to the unpredictable nature of their charges.

Thus, the complexities of life at the Gary Job Corps Center during this tumultuous period reveal a multifaceted struggle for autonomy, safety, and respect amidst an environment rife with challenges.

CHAPTER FOURTEEN: PROFOUND TRANSFORMATION

In the aftermath of the tornado that devastated the Gary Job Corps Center, a profound transformation unfolded within the community, one that transcended the immediate physical destruction and delved into the very essence of human resilience and solidarity. The catastrophic events, marked by buildings submerged in water and the heartbreaking loss of students' belongings, catalyzed an unprecedented unity among both students and staff. This collective endeavor to restore what had been lost not only fostered a sense of camaraderie but also illuminated the capacity for empathy and altruism. Individuals who had previously been at odds found common ground in their shared struggle for survival.

The environment, once fraught with behavioral challenges, shifted dramatically. The urgency of the situation eclipsed past grievances, allowing for a rare moment of harmony. In this context, even the most troubled students emerged as unexpected leaders, demonstrating that, under the direst circumstances, the innate human capacity for compassion can prevail over previous animosities, irrespective of race or background. Such instances of solidarity served as a testament to the transformative power of adversity, revealing that the true measure of a community lies not in its challenges but in its ability to rise above them.

The transition from a conventional security framework to the involvement of federal law enforcement underscored the gravity of the situation and the community's response to the perceived threat posed by the students. While the citizens of San Marcos exhibited a palpable disdain for the Gary students, their reliance on the labor provided by these individuals for economic sustenance created a complex dynamic. The juxtaposition of community resentment and economic dependency illustrated the nuanced relationship between societal perceptions and the realities of rehabilitation efforts.

The challenges faced by the Gary Job Corps Center in monitoring student behavior highlighted the inherent difficulties in managing a population that, once dispersed, often eluded oversight. This situation necessitated a reevaluation of strategies employed to foster positive behavior, as the traditional methods proved inadequate in the face of such widespread dislocation. The implications of these circumstances extended beyond the immediate context, prompting a broader discourse on the efficacy of rehabilitation programs and the societal structures that support or hinder their success.

Ultimately, the events that unfolded at the Gary Job Corps Center served as a microcosm of the broader human experience, wherein adversity could catalyze profound change, revealing the potential for growth and understanding amidst chaos. This narrative not only reflected the resilience of the human spirit but also invited a critical examination of the systems in place that govern responses to such crises.

In reflecting upon his experiences with students, it became evident that the transformative journey he witnessed was not merely a series of isolated incidents; rather, it represented a profound shift in the educational landscape, characterized by notable improvements in graduation rates and a marked decrease in violence. This metamorphosis was catalyzed by instilling in students a sense of purpose, enabling them to recognize their potential for greatness. He endeavored to teach them that their past should not serve as a crutch for failure but rather as a foundation upon which they could build their aspirations for excellence.

Moreover, he took it upon himself to engage with those students who were often marginalized, those whom others deemed unworthy of investment. He worked to mold them into leaders imbued with a sense of responsibility and ambition. By fostering an environment that emphasized self-respect and pride, remarkable transformations emerged; students who once languished in the shadows began to ascend to new heights, surpassing even the expectations of their peers and educators alike.

After dedicating eight years to this mission, his efforts culminated in an interview with esteemed campus managers, including Harvey Miller, Sheppard, Ward, Lynn Banks, and Supervisor Joe T. Bell. This pivotal moment led to his promotion to center supervisor, a role that entailed comprehensive oversight of the center's operations across four campuses and an honors dormitory. The responsibilities associated with this position were substantial, as he was tasked with the daily supervision of all staff within the residential living area, underscoring the weight of the trust placed in him.

The endorsement Arthur received from then-US Congressman Bill Patman, communicated electronically from Washington, DC, served as a testament to his successful contributions during the congressman's reelection campaign in the Washington County, Texas, area. However, it soon became apparent that Arthur's tenure at Gary was approaching an unforeseen conclusion, precipitated by the intricate dynamics of political maneuvering that he had no desire to engage in. The realization of the underhanded tactics employed by certain individuals in key management positions, driven by their own agendas, illuminated the precarious nature of his situation and foreshadowed the challenges that lay ahead.

In the beginning, Arthur's experiences with students were profoundly transformative, as he witnessed significant changes in their academic performance and behavioral conduct, notably a marked decrease in violence and an increase in graduation rates. This evolution was not merely coincidental; rather, it stemmed from instilling in them a sense of purpose and the understanding that they possessed the potential to surpass their own expectations. He endeavored to teach the students to utilize their past experiences not as a debilitating crutch but as a powerful catalyst for excellence.

Arthur focused on those students who had been marginalized and often overlooked by both their peers and educators. Through dedicated mentorship, he was able to cultivate their latent leadership qualities, instilling in them a sense of responsibility and the ambition to set and achieve higher goals. The transformation he observed was nothing short of remarkable; students who once struggled began to ascend to new heights, surprising not only themselves but also the faculty and administration.

After eight years of dedicated service, Arthur's efforts culminated in an interview with campus managers — Sheppard, Ward, Lynn Banks, and Supervisor Joe T. Bell — resulting in his promotion to center supervisor. This role encompassed the comprehensive oversight of daily operations across four campuses and an honors dormitory, a position that demanded not only leadership but also a profound commitment to fostering an environment conducive to student success.

His appointment was further validated by a recommendation from then-US Congressman Bill Patman, who acknowledged Arthur's contributions during the reelection campaign. However, as he ascended to this new role, he became acutely aware of the political machines at play within the institution.

The realization that his tenure at Gary was approaching an abrupt conclusion due to the underhanded maneuverings of certain individuals in management was both disheartening and enlightening. This experience underscored the complexities of educational leadership, where personal ambition often intersected with institutional politics, revealing the intricate dynamics that governed such environments.

The staff at the wellness center were, however, just as corrupt as the staff in residential living; one had to be part of the inner circle to secure benefits that fostered growth and progress within that department. On numerous occasions, the staff attempted to manipulate Geraldine, using her as a pawn in their schemes while simultaneously attributing to her responsibilities for circumstances beyond her control — a tactic they employed to evade accountability.

The supervisor during that period epitomized duplicity, presenting a facade of congeniality while covertly undermining those who were unsuspecting. Many of her coworkers were friends only by convenience, their alliances fragile and transactional. Nevertheless, Geraldine maintained her integrity, treating them with the utmost respect and cooperating fully in her professional duties.

At the end of each day, Geraldine returned home, and despite any feelings of despondence stemming from her work environment, she adeptly compartmentalized her emotions, embodying the role of a devoted mother and wife. The ritual of sharing the day's events with her family served as a therapeutic outlet, transforming the burdens of the day into shared experiences that fortified their familial bonds. Geraldine's character was marked by even-mindedness; she was quiet yet perceptive, choosing to remain uninvolved in the personal affairs of others, thereby ensuring that she upheld her reputation as a diligent and principled worker both in her professional and domestic spheres.

Despite her unwavering commitment to the Job Corps program, Geraldine found herself consistently overlooked, underpaid, and disregarded, even by the management of the Texas Educational Foundation. However, a significant transformation occurred after approximately five years of dedicated service. Geraldine evolved into a master of her craft as a medical technician alongside Gary.

As time progressed, she ascended to the roles of wellness center shift leader and center pregnancy coordinator and frequently assumed the responsibilities of health service administrator under both the Texas Educational Foundation and, later, the Management and Training Corporation, the new contractor for the center. Geraldine's journey exemplifies resilience and the pursuit of excellence in the face of systemic challenges.

CHAPTER FIFTEEN: PRIOR FILINGS

The overwhelming number of complaints prompted significant intervention, leading to the involvement of the local NAACP president. According to a representative from the Department of Labor for the Texas Job Corps Region, this escalation ultimately resulted in the consideration and subsequent termination of the labor contract with the Department of Labor for the Texas Educational Foundation Inc., which had been responsible for operating the local Job Corps center. The troubled contractor, having managed the Gary Job Corps from its inception in 1964 until 2000, was on the verge of becoming a historical footnote.

This transition heralded a dramatic transformation within the Gary Job Corps program. The contract for its operation became available for negotiation, allowing other companies nationwide that met governmental criteria the opportunity to submit bids for the project.

The operational control of the center transitioned from the Texas Educational Foundation to the Management and Training Corporation, a for-profit entity based in Utah, marking a significant shift from nonprofit management. Upon notification of this change in leadership, all staff members were placed on alert regarding the impending alterations in the management structure of the center. This incited a wave of unrest among employees.

Initially, many staff members expressed enthusiasm at the prospect of forthcoming changes, viewing them as a potential remedy for what had devolved into a dysfunctional operation. The level of motivation surged to unprecedented heights, as this excitement reflected a burgeoning hope that the new employer would foster an environment conducive to improvement, enhancing both advancement opportunities and income levels for all involved.

However, this initial optimism soon gave way to apprehension. Staff members began to fear for their job security amidst the sweeping changes in policies and procedures, as well as shifts in their professional status. For the majority, the departure of the Texas Educational Foundation was met with relief, yet the uncertainty surrounding the new management instigated a complex emotional landscape, oscillating between hope and anxiety regarding the future of the center and its personnel.

This transition marked a pivotal moment in the operational dynamics of the Gary Job Corps program. The contract to manage the center became subject to competitive bidding, inviting various companies nationwide that met governmental criteria to vie for the opportunity. Ultimately, the Management and Training Corporation (MTC), hailing from Utah, assumed control of the center, signifying a shift from a nonprofit management model to one driven by profit motives.

The transition precipitated a wave of anxiety among the staff, who were formally notified of the impending changes in management, leading to a palpable sense of unrest throughout the facility. The staff's apprehension was rooted in fears of job insecurity, potential alterations in established policies and procedures, and an overall shift in their professional status.

Despite this, a segment of the workforce expressed optimism regarding the departure of the Texas Educational Foundation, believing that the new management could herald a positive transformation for the center. Upon MTC's arrival, the atmosphere was characterized by unprecedented confusion as employees grappled with the uncertainties of their employment status.

A salient inquiry posed to the medical staff — *Have any of you pushed to keep your employment?* — elicited a unanimous silence, underscoring the pervasive uncertainty that enveloped the center. When Geraldine returned from her interview with MTC, her acceptance into the nursing position offered a glimmer of hope amidst the chaos. Similarly, Glenda Steen retained her role as the senior secretary in the wellness center, providing a measure of stability in an otherwise tumultuous environment.

The prevailing sentiment among the staff was one of anticipation. They harbored expectations that the introduction of a new management entity would translate into enhanced financial resources, improved compensation, and superior benefits. However, the initial weeks following MTC's takeover were marked by discernible unrest as the staff navigated the complexities of the transition and awaited clarity regarding their roles and futures within the newly structured organization.

This period of adjustment was undoubtedly a formidable challenge for MTC as they endeavored to establish order and coherence in the wake of such significant operational changes.

In the beginning, it became increasingly apparent that the Management and Training Corporation (MTC) was ill-prepared to comprehend the vastness and complexity of the Gary Job Corps Center, a facility that not only housed an extensive array of residential living quarters — twenty-two in total — but also boasted an impressive infrastructure comprising over one hundred educational, training, and administrative buildings.

The sheer scale of the center, which included a dining service, gymnasium, pool hall, church, a comprehensive transportation department, a security center, and a newly established wellness center dedicated to the late Congressman J. J. Pickle, posed significant challenges for MTC management. They appeared bewildered and disoriented in the face of issues they had not encountered at other centers.

The Gary facility was equipped with an emergency room, two ambulances, and a diverse team of medical professionals, including technicians, nurses, doctors, specialists, psychologists, psychiatrists, and drug counselors, all of whom played a crucial role in the effective treatment of students. This state-of-the-art wellness center surpassed the capabilities of any other segment of the center, underscoring the magnitude of the undertaking. Furthermore, the transportation center featured its own gas station, a driver's education program, and offerings such as GED preparation and vocational training, all of which contributed to a comprehensive support system for the students.

During the initial tour, MTC representatives struggled to assimilate the extensive array of services provided by the dedicated staff, leading to a palpable sense of confusion. As one newcomer aptly remarked, *"We call it a city within a city,"* highlighting the center's self-sufficient nature, which included staff housing comprising over one hundred units, as well as separate accommodations for executive management.

Geraldine, a seasoned staff member, was frequently called upon to assist the new management in strategic planning, facilitating their acclimatization to a system of such magnitude that it necessitated the collective expertise and experience of all involved.

As time progressed, discontent among the staff began to surface, with whispers of impending job cuts and the likelihood of departures becoming increasingly common. The Management Training staff's presence, while intended to provide guidance, only served to exacerbate the uncertainty, leaving many to question the sustainability of the center's operations amidst the looming challenges.

The introduction of the Management and Training Corporation (MTC) at the Gary Job Corps Center marked a significant turning point, characterized by a series of detrimental decisions that profoundly impacted both the staff and the students. The abrupt reduction of personnel, coupled with interference in the educational program, resulted in the hiring of inadequately trained staff across various cities and centers. This mismanagement extended to the placement of individuals in roles for which they possessed neither the requisite knowledge nor the experience, thereby undermining the quality of care and education that had previously been established.

It became evident that MTC had underestimated the level of medical care provided to the students and the extensive capabilities of the hospital located within the center. A pivotal moment occurred when management, upon finally visiting the facility, was struck by the realization of the comprehensive services available, a stark contrast to their prior assumptions. The wellness staff at Gary Job Corps Center demonstrated exceptional proficiency in addressing medical issues, ensuring that students received effective treatment and consistently improved under their care. Indeed, it is posited that the quality of medical attention offered to students at the center surpassed that of the local hospital, a testament to the expertise and dedication of the medical team.

However, the introduction of MTC precipitated a troubling trend characterized by a high turnover rate among staff, which fostered an environment rife with uncertainty and anxiety. This revolving door of employment not only inflicted emotional distress upon the employees but also engendered a pervasive fear regarding their financial stability and future prospects.

Many staff members found themselves grappling with an emotional roller coaster, exacerbated by the unpredictable nature of management decisions that could result in sudden job loss for any number of reasons.

As MTC's influence grew, a wave of complaints began to circulate among the staff, albeit in hushed tones. Accusations regarding unprofessional conduct by management, particularly in relation to female staff members, emerged as a significant concern. Whether these allegations were substantiated or not, they reflected a broader atmosphere of distrust and discontent as employees shared their experiences and observations, often tinged with apprehension. The environment became increasingly toxic, marked by a culture of deceit and misconduct, which ultimately eroded the morale and cohesion of the workforce.

The narrative surrounding employment, financial struggles, and the emotional toll of uncertainty presents a profound exploration of human experience, particularly within the context of young adulthood. This story delves into the complexities faced by individuals navigating the precarious balance of work, education, and familial responsibilities, as exemplified by the experiences of Geraldine and her partner during a tumultuous period of their lives.

CHAPTER SIXTEEN: CONTEXTUAL BACKGROUND

In the early stages of Geraldine's employment, a palpable sense of anxiety permeated the atmosphere, particularly regarding her safety in the workplace. This concern was exacerbated by a brief yet unsettling encounter with several students, raising questions about the security measures in place at her place of employment. The precariousness of her situation mirrored Geraldine's partner's own circumstances, characterized by a lack of financial stability and the pressing need for employment. The anticipation of a job offer from the center became a source of both hope and despair as the days turned into weeks without any communication regarding the status of the application.

Financial Struggles and Emotional Toll

The financial strain experienced by young couples, particularly those who are married and pursuing education, cannot be overstated. Geraldine's partner reflected on the challenges of being young, married, and financially constrained—challenges that were not anticipated at the onset but became a constant response to their external journey.

The burden of managing monthly expenses, particularly in light of the limited financial support provided by VA education benefits, created a sense of urgency and desperation. The stark reality of rummaging through a food pantry, only to find the meager offerings of bread and Miracle Whip, served as a poignant illustration of the struggles faced during this period. Geraldine, as the primary breadwinner, bore the weight of these financial responsibilities, which undoubtedly added to the emotional strain on both partners.

Turning Point: Job Interview

After a prolonged period of uncertainty, a glimmer of hope emerged when Geraldine's partner received a call regarding the application status at Gary. The elation experienced upon being invited for an interview marked a significant turning point, shifting the tone from despair to optimism.

The anticipation of the interview, coupled with the desire to secure a position in the security department, underscored the importance of employment in alleviating financial burdens. However, the eventual hiring into residential living, rather than the anticipated security role, highlighted the unpredictable nature of job markets and the necessity of adaptability in the face of unforeseen circumstances.

Reflections on Resilience

The experiences of Geraldine and her partner encapsulate the myriad challenges faced by young individuals striving for stability amidst financial and emotional turmoil. The narrative illustrates not only the struggles inherent in balancing work, education, and familial obligations but also the resilience that emerges in the face of adversity.

As they navigated the complexities of their situation, the eventual job offer served as a beacon of hope, reinforcing the notion that perseverance and adaptability are crucial in overcoming life's obstacles. *What choice did we have but to keep pushing forward?*

Ultimately, this account serves as a testament to the human spirit's capacity to endure and thrive, even in the most challenging of circumstances.

As Geraldine assumed the role of the right hand to several regular supervisors, she found herself entrusted with the oversight of nine dormitories, which collectively housed up to 120 students at any given time. Additionally, she managed up to 18 staff members during peak shifts, specifically from two-thirty in the afternoon until midnight.

This position not only represented the largest operational responsibility among the four campuses within the center but also underscored the significant expectations placed upon any residential advisor or campus supervisor. The late Joe Garcia, the campus manager, exemplified a stringent approach to accountability, embodying a no-nonsense managerial style that resonated throughout the institution. Similarly, the direct-line campus supervisor, Don Edwards, mirrored this commitment to excellence, demanding high-quality performance from both staff and students alike.

Don Edwards, a self-proclaimed workaholic, possessed an extensive understanding of Department of Labor standards, which he diligently enforced through a framework of rules and regulations that established elevated expectations for daily conduct. Observing his methods closely, Geraldine endeavored to emulate his approach, equipping herself to uphold these standards within her own residence, thereby fostering an environment conducive to both staff and student accountability.

In a pivotal moment during Geraldine's tenure, following the departure of the residential counselor, she found herself stepping into the role of acting counselor while simultaneously fulfilling her regular duties across three campus areas. These responsibilities included liaising with campus supervisors and managing additional tasks related to student trades and class accountability. This experience illuminated a critical lesson: despite the challenging behavior exhibited by students under the auspices of the Texas Educational Foundation, the nonprofit entity operating under the US Department of Labor, their academic engagement remained commendable. The students not only attended classes but excelled in their respective trades, a testament to the faculty's adeptness in imparting knowledge and skills essential for their development.

At one point, Geraldine was assigned exclusively to work with criminal-minded youth residing in her facility—individuals who had typically been placed there by the judicial system. Under her supervision, the likelihood of these young individuals reforming and pursuing a more constructive path became significantly more attainable. Her subsequent experiences with students were transformative; she witnessed remarkable changes manifested in improved graduation rates and a notable decrease in violent incidents.

This evolution was not coincidental; it stemmed from an eagerness to effectuate positive change. These students were imbued with a newfound sense of purpose, provided with compelling reasons to aspire to excellence, and encouraged to believe they could surpass even the highest expectations of themselves. *What if they could truly become better than their past?*

In her pedagogical approach, Geraldine emphasized the importance of utilizing their past experiences not as a crutch for failure but rather as a catalyst for personal growth and achievement. She took on the challenge of mentoring students whom others deemed unworthy of attention or care, transforming them into leaders equipped with genuine responsibilities and tangible goals. By instilling higher expectations, she nurtured their self-respect and self-pride, catalyzing a profound shift in their trajectories.

The progress she observed in these young lives was not only gratifying but also astonishing, leaving an indelible impression on all involved.

After eight years of dedicated service and following a rigorous interview process with the campus managers, Geraldine was honored with a promotion to center supervisor. This role entailed comprehensive oversight of the daily operations across four campuses and an honors dormitory. As the center supervisor, she bore significant responsibility for all daytime staff within the residential living area, a position that demanded both leadership and accountability.

A pivotal moment in Geraldine's career was marked by a recommendation she received via electronic communication from Washington, DC, from then-US Congressman Bill Patman. This endorsement was a direct result of her successful contributions to his reelection campaign and that of Former Speaker of the Texas House of Representatives, County Judge Gus Mutchler, within the Washington County, Texas area. The campaign achieved the largest voter turnout in Washington County history, further solidifying her commitment to public service and community development.

It was at this juncture that the trajectory of her professional journey became unmistakably clear, revealing the profound impact that dedicated mentorship and leadership can have on the lives of young individuals.

While it was commendable that over 90 percent of employees expressed their willingness to support the union, it was crucial to recognize the formidable influence that management exerted. This influence ultimately culminated in a singular vote that thwarted the center's aspirations for unionization in Texas. The revelation of Geraldine's connections to Washington, particularly her association with the former Texas Speaker of the House of Representatives—stemming from her vigorous efforts in his reelection campaign for the county judgeship in Washington County—served as a catalyst for management's retaliatory tactics.

These tactics, which manifested in the denial of her promotion, were emblematic of a broader strategy aimed at undermining her professional trajectory as a form of retribution for her advocacy. Consequently, the decision to seek new opportunities became not only a necessity but also a welcome reprieve from the pervasive political strife that characterized the workplace environment.

The circumstances surrounding Geraldine's departure were particularly disheartening, as she was compelled to resign on the very day her promotion was ostensibly granted. This outcome was predicated on spurious allegations and unfounded accusations, transparently designed to facilitate the ascension of a preferred candidate. This period was fraught with challenges, especially as Geraldine grappled with setbacks and corruption within her department. However, her resilience was a testament to her character.

The emotional toll of leaving a position she had come to cherish was exacerbated by the financial implications of unemployment, particularly with the arrival of a newborn child. The director's rude and negative demeanor, which was likened to the elementary-minded thinking that often belied his professional conduct, further compounded the difficulties Geraldine faced.

Despite the adversities, Geraldine's tenure at the center was marked by meaningful interactions with students from whom she derived as much learning as they did from the program. Thus, the decision to move forward was not merely a response to external pressure but also a reflection of her desire to pursue a more fulfilling and appreciative professional landscape.

CHAPTER SEVENTEEN: COMPLAINTS

The overwhelming number of complaints prompted the involvement of the local NAACP president, which, as conveyed in a personal conversation with a representative from the Department of Labor for the Texas Job Corps Region, ultimately led to the consideration and subsequent termination of the labor contract with the Department of Labor for the Texas Educational Foundation Inc. in the operation of the local Job Corps center. This marked a significant turning point, as the troubled contractor, having operated the Gary Job Corps from 1964 to 2000, was on the verge of becoming a historical footnote.

The contract for the center was opened for negotiations, allowing various companies across the nation that met government requirements to submit bids for the Job Corps Center project. Consequently, the operational control transitioned from Gary to the Management and Training Corporation (MTC) based in Utah, shifting from a nonprofit management model to a profit-driven operational framework.

Upon notification of this leadership change, all staff members were placed on alert regarding the impending modifications in management, which instigated a wave of unrest throughout the center. Initially, many employees expressed enthusiasm regarding the forthcoming changes, viewing them as a potential remedy for what had been perceived as a dysfunctional operation. The heightened level of motivation among the staff was unprecedented, reflecting a renewed sense of hope that the new employer would foster an environment conducive to improvement, thereby enhancing both advancement opportunities and income potential.

However, this optimism was soon tempered by the looming fear of job loss, coupled with anticipated major alterations in policies and procedures, as well as shifts in employee status. For the majority, the departure of the Texas Educational Foundation was met with relief, as the prospect of a new management structure was anticipated to herald a transformative era for the center. The atmosphere within the center was characterized by an unprecedented level of confusion and anxiety, a phenomenon that had not been observed in years.

The pivotal inquiry posed to the medical staff — *Have any of you pushed to keep your employment?* — elicited a profound silence, as none were willing to voice their concerns amidst the uncertainty of impending interviews. Geraldine's subsequent acceptance of the nursing position at MTC marked a significant turning point; however, it did little to alleviate the pervasive unrest that enveloped the remaining staff. Glenda

Steen's retention of her role as senior secretary in the wellness center provided a semblance of stability, yet the overarching sentiment was one of trepidation regarding the future.

The staff harbored the hope that the introduction of a new management operator would herald improvements in financial remuneration and benefits. Nevertheless, the transition to MTC was fraught with challenges, as the complexities of integrating a new management structure while the previous company was still in the process of vacating created a palpable tension. This period of adjustment was not merely a logistical hurdle for MTC; it also necessitated a delicate balancing act to maintain operational continuity within the center.

In light of these challenges, the existing staff, many of whom had extensive experience, assumed a proactive role in facilitating the transition by imparting their knowledge to the incoming MTC personnel. Geraldine was approached by the new management to assist with various projects, a task she undertook with commendable enthusiasm and dedication. However, the environment was further complicated by rampant gossip and speculation, which served to exacerbate the already heightened tensions among the staff.

The pervasive culture of distrust led to a survivalist mentality, where individuals resorted to undermining their colleagues in a desperate bid to secure their positions. The resultant atmosphere was one of palpable despair, reminiscent of the societal struggles witnessed during the Great Depression, where the instinct for self-preservation overshadowed collective solidarity.

This scenario underscores the profound impact of organizational change on employee morale and highlights the intricate dynamics of human behavior in the face of uncertainty and competition. The initial optimism surrounding the arrival of the new management team began to wane, revealing a more complex and nuanced reality.

The perception that the influx of resources and personnel would lead to significant improvements in the operational efficiency of the transportation center was soon overshadowed by the palpable tension among the existing staff. As the newcomers, equipped with their ostentatious displays of authority and financial resources, attempted to impose their vision, a sense of disillusionment permeated the atmosphere.

Furthermore, the juxtaposition of the newcomers' lavish spending against the backdrop of impending job cuts created an environment rife with uncertainty and anxiety. The phrase *city within a city* aptly encapsulated the insular nature of the center, yet it also highlighted the disconnect between the management's aspirations and the realities faced by the staff. The existing employees, who had dedicated years to the center, found themselves grappling with the implications of a management style that prioritized external appearances over the intrinsic value of their contributions.

In addition, the comments made by the new managers, particularly the derogatory remarks about the local staff, served to exacerbate the divide. Such statements not only reflected a lack of respect for the existing workforce but also underscored a broader issue of cultural insensitivity that often accompanied the introduction of new leadership. The existing staff, who had cultivated a deep understanding of the center's operations and community dynamics, were left feeling marginalized and undervalued.

Consequently, the initial excitement surrounding the new management's arrival transformed into a critical examination of their approach. The staff's observations regarding the management's spending habits and their perceived disconnect from the realities of the center highlighted a significant challenge: the need for a more integrative and respectful management strategy that acknowledges and leverages the expertise of long-standing employees.

As the situation evolved, it became increasingly clear that the success of the transportation center would hinge not on the superficial changes implemented by the new management but rather on their ability to foster collaboration and mutual respect among all staff members. The reluctance of staff members to report their concerns to higher authorities could be attributed to a pervasive culture of fear and self-preservation, exacerbated by the hierarchical dynamics within the organization.

The responses of individuals, such as the succinct yet revealing statements, *I will lose my job* or *I cannot afford to lose my job,* underscored the profound anxiety that permeated the workplace environment. This fear was not merely a personal concern; it reflected a systemic issue where the potential for job loss or humiliation acted as a powerful deterrent against speaking out.

Furthermore, the phenomenon of sycophantic behavior among the staff, characterized by the "kiss-up-to-me" campaign, illustrated the lengths to which individuals would go to secure their positions. This behavior not only undermined the integrity of the workplace but also perpetuated a toxic atmosphere where genuine concerns were silenced in favor of appeasing management. The practice of reporting on colleagues, often based on trivial or unfounded grievances, served as a mechanism for management to exert control, fostering an environment rife with distrust and competition rather than collaboration.

The optimism expressed by Geraldine and other staff members regarding potential changes within the center reflected a desire for improvement in working conditions and organizational practices.

However, this hope was juxtaposed against the stark reality of MTC management's ignorance, which became increasingly apparent.

The absurdity of the staff's adulation for management, epitomized by the ceremonial greetings and the playful yet demeaning song, *Hail to the Chief,* revealed a troubling dynamic where respect was conflated with blind obedience. In this context, the director's perceived authority as a "mighty giant" ultimately faded, masking the limitations of his actual influence over the center's operations.

The realization that such behavior was not only counterproductive but also indicative of a deeper malaise within the organization prompted a critical examination of the underlying power structures at play. This situation necessitated a reevaluation of the organizational culture, advocating for a shift towards transparency and accountability, where staff could voice their concerns without fear of retribution.

In contemplating the intricate dynamics of societal discourse, it became evident that the right to individual choice was paramount; however, the implications of such autonomy necessitated a critical examination of the sources from which information was derived. The dialogue with Mr. Taylor underscored a profound truth: the veracity of information was often obscured by subjective interpretation. His admonition to *open your eyes and your ears* served as a compelling reminder of the necessity for vigilance in discerning truth amidst the cacophony of opinions that permeated the social fabric.

The post office in San Marcos, as a microcosm of communal interaction, exemplified the duality of human nature — wherein the sharing of gossip could simultaneously foster connection and perpetuate misinformation. This phenomenon was not merely anecdotal; it reflected a broader societal tendency to engage in collective narratives that lacked empirical substantiation. The barbershop, too, emerged as a critical site for the exchange of experiences, particularly concerning the challenges faced by African American employees within the Gary Job Corps system.

The reluctance of individuals to confront systemic issues, as highlighted in the narratives shared, revealed a pervasive culture of fear that stifled open dialogue and hindered progress. Moreover, the observation regarding the management practices at Gary Job Corps invited a nuanced analysis of leadership dynamics within racially diverse contexts.

The assertion that Black management represented a decline in operational efficacy compared to the Texas Educational Foundation (TEF) raised significant questions about the intersection of race, authority, and organizational culture. Under TEF, employees reportedly experienced a clearer understanding of their roles, which contrasted sharply with the ambiguity and discontent that emerged under subsequent leadership. This disparity reflected the complexities of institutional governance and underscored the critical need for equitable and effective management practices that empowered all employees, irrespective of their racial or ethnic backgrounds.

In summary, the interplay of personal narratives and systemic challenges within the Gary Job Corps context illuminated the broader societal issues of communication, leadership, and the quest for truth. As these multifaceted realities were navigated, fostering an environment where open dialogue was encouraged and diverse perspectives were valued became imperative, enabling a more profound understanding of the complexities that defined the collective experience.

The historical context of the "good-ole-boy" system revealed a pervasive culture of ignorance and complicity within management structures, particularly exemplified by the actions of center director

Lonnie Hall, colloquially referred to as "Mr. One Glove." This moniker, derived from his peculiar fashion choice of wearing a single glove, served as a metaphor for the superficiality of his leadership style, which was characterized by a lack of transparency and accountability.

Hall's strategic maneuvering to undermine veteran staff members while simultaneously concealing his intentions behind the fade of white management underscored a profound ethical deficiency that jeopardized workforce morale and perpetuated systemic inequities. The transition in management, ostensibly aimed at revitalizing the center, instead revealed an underlying agenda that marginalized experienced personnel in favor of less qualified individuals.

This shift, ostensibly sanctioned by Black management, raised critical questions regarding the criteria for leadership selection and the implications of such decisions on institutional integrity. The historical significance of the center, once championed by figures such as President Lyndon Baines Johnson and Congressman J. J. Pickle, was juxtaposed against these troubling developments, leading to an alarming increase in legal consultations among disaffected employees seeking redress for perceived injustices.

Consequently, the initial complaints, which may have appeared trivial, evolved into a clarion call for systemic reform, reflecting deeper issues that demanded urgent attention. The wellness center administration, while grappling with its own growing pains, was compelled to confront the ramifications of its decisions and the broader implications for the community it served. This situation necessitated a thorough examination of the policies and practices governing management behavior, alongside a commitment to fostering an environment where all employees felt valued and empowered to contribute meaningfully to the organization's mission.

CHAPTER EIGHTEEN: DISCRIMINATION IS COMMONPLACE

In examining the transition from the previous administration to the arrival of the Management Training Company (MTC), it becomes evident that the foundational ethos established by the old management was instrumental in fostering a culture of achievement and resilience among students. The unwavering commitment to academic success, exemplified by the rigorous attendance policies and the emphasis on obtaining a General Educational Development (GED) certificate, not only provided students with essential skills but also instilled a sense of pride and accomplishment.

Furthermore, the emergence of student leaders during this period highlights the transformative potential of educational institutions when they prioritize student engagement and empowerment. These individuals, who aspired to transcend their circumstances, serve as a testament to the notion that, with the right support, even those deemed 'at-risk' can flourish and contribute positively to their communities. Consequently, the narrative of the center during this era is not merely one of challenges and defiance; rather, it is a story of hope, resilience, and the profound capacity for change that resides within every individual.

As MTC took the reins, it became crucial to reflect on the legacy of the previous administration and the foundational principles that must be preserved to ensure the center continues to serve as a beacon of opportunity for future generations. However, the period from 2004 to November 2005 was marked by a significant decline in the internal growth and development of staff work products, attributed to a confluence of factors, including a notable lack of commitment to organizational goals.

This deterioration was, in part, a consequence of insufficient support and direction from senior management, compounded by ineffective leadership practices that fostered an environment of staff abuse. Communication channels between MTC management and human resources were predominantly unidirectional, resulting in profound neglect of the feelings and needs of subordinates, which were not only overlooked but also disrespected.

The parties involved, particularly senior management at the MTC center, played a pivotal role in engendering a climate of fear regarding job security, personal well-being, and self-esteem. This atmosphere of intimidation was perpetuated by management's failure to address numerous complaints related to Equal Employment Opportunity Commission (EEOC) issues. The persistent inaction of senior center management in failing to investigate these complaints and the urgent pleas from staff for intervention exemplified a stark absence of supportive leadership.

Moreover, the directives issued by MTC center management and wellness center management contributed to the phenomenon of "role conflict." This was primarily due to the imposition of excessive duties upon staff, which were inherently unmanageable within the constraints of their existing roles and compensation. The management's inability to clearly delineate the responsibilities of the wellness center and other staff members, coupled with a lack of adequate training in accordance with newly instituted policies, represented a fundamental failure in leadership practices that should have been standard at the Gary facility.

Consequently, wellness and other center staff were compelled to operate with a severely limited number of trained personnel, often shouldering additional responsibilities to ensure the center's functionality and adherence to the standards mandated by the U.S. Department of Labor. This situation was exacerbated by the involvement of personnel who lacked the requisite training for the job-course environment, further undermining the overall efficacy of the center's operations.

The pervasive issues surrounding workplace conduct and the subsequent ramifications for staff morale and performance at the Gary Job Corps Center cannot be overstated. The allegations articulated in the federal EEOC complaints filed in 2004 and 2005 highlight a troubling pattern of behavior exhibited by certain administrators, notably Ms. Smith and Ms. Benson, which starkly contrasts with the expectations of professional conduct.

While it is acknowledged that various wellness center administrators have cycled through the facility, each with their own interpretations of disciplinary measures, the detrimental impact of their actions on staff cannot be dismissed. The staff's unwavering commitment to delivering high-quality service to the student body was undermined by a toxic work environment, exacerbated by the vindictive behavior of individuals such as Mary Beth Magovsky. This hostility not only stifled open communication but also compelled employees like Geraldine and Glenda to seek recourse through external authorities, fully aware of the potential repercussions from management.

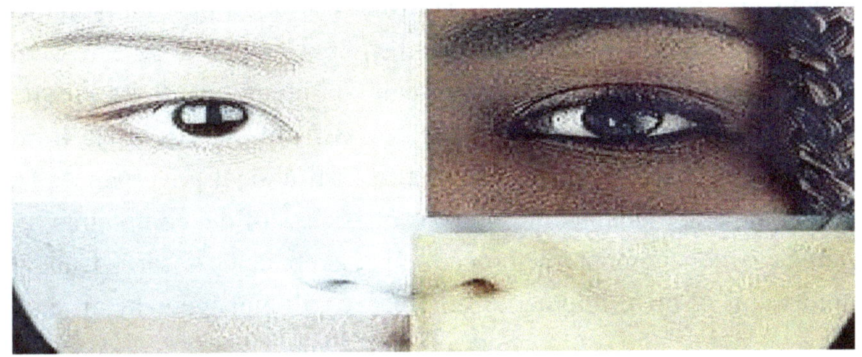

The legal framework surrounding workplace harassment, particularly as it pertains to race, ethnicity, or national origin, underscores the gravity of these allegations. The courts have established that victims of such discrimination possess the right to pursue legal action against their employers. Furthermore, the EEOC policy stipulates that management bears a responsibility to either address or be aware of discriminatory conduct within the workplace.

The failure of MTC management, exemplified by the actions of senior management center director Lonnie Hall, to adequately respond to these issues not only reflects a systemic disregard for employee welfare but also suggests an implicit endorsement of such behavior. Consequently, the notion that management condones harassment and discrimination becomes increasingly evident, raising profound questions about the ethical standards upheld within the organization.

This situation serves as a critical reminder of the necessity for robust policies and practices that prioritize the dignity and rights of all employees, thereby fostering a more equitable and supportive work environment.

Dynamics of Communication

In the realm of organizational management, particularly within educational institutions such as the MTC/Gary Job Corps Center, the dynamics of communication and conflict resolution play a pivotal role in maintaining an effective operational environment. The case involving Taylor and Steen, as documented in their complaints and the subsequent rebuttals to the accusations levied by Benson, serves as a salient example of the complexities inherent in institutional governance. This account aims to elucidate the significant aspects of the complaints filed against the management, the procedural discrepancies observed, and the implications of these interactions on the overall management structure.

The MTC/Gary Job Corps Center, tasked with providing vocational training and support to at-risk youth, operates under a framework that necessitates adherence to established policies and procedures. However, the issuance of a letter of concern, as opposed to a letter of caution, raises questions regarding the procedural integrity of the management's response mechanisms. This distinction is not merely semantic; it reflects a deeper systemic issue that undermines the principles of fairness and transparency that should govern such institutions. The implications of this misstep extend beyond individual grievances, potentially affecting the morale and trust of the staff and students alike.

Documentation of Complaints

The complaints articulated by Taylor and Steen were meticulously documented, serving as a formal record of their grievances against the management's actions. The primary contention revolved around the perceived inadequacies in the management's response to their concerns, which they argued were not only unwarranted but also indicative of a broader pattern of mismanagement.

The documentation included specific instances where the management failed to adhere to established protocols, thereby exacerbating the situation rather than facilitating a resolution. This paper trail was deemed essential, not merely for the sake of accountability but also as a safeguard against potential retaliatory actions that could arise from their complaints.

Rebuttals to Accusations

In addressing the accusations made by Benson, it became evident that a robust rebuttal was necessary to challenge the validity of the claims and uphold the integrity of the complainants. The rebuttals were crafted with a focus on presenting a systematic and evidence-based response, highlighting inconsistencies in Benson's assertions and emphasizing the procedural lapses that had occurred.

Furthermore, the rebuttals underscored the importance of adhering to the center's policies and procedures, which were ostensibly designed to protect the rights and interests of both staff and students. The challenge posed by these accusations not only required a defense of personal integrity but also necessitated a broader critique of the management's operational practices.

Management's Response and Challenges

Despite the concerted efforts by Geraldine and Glenda to engage the center management in a constructive dialogue aimed at resolution, the response from key management personnel was notably inadequate. The reluctance to address the issues raised by Taylor and Steen highlighted a significant barrier to effective communication and conflict resolution within the organization.

This lack of responsiveness not only perpetuated the grievances but also fostered an environment of distrust and disillusionment among the staff. The failure to take appropriate actions in response to the documented complaints raises critical questions about the efficacy of the management structure and its commitment to fostering a supportive and equitable workplace.

Implications for Future Management Practices

The unfolding events surrounding the complaints and rebuttals at the MTC/Gary Job Corps Center serve as a cautionary tale for organizational management. The necessity of establishing clear communication channels and adhering to procedural guidelines cannot be overstated, as these elements are fundamental to maintaining a healthy organizational culture.

Furthermore, the implications of this case extend beyond the immediate context, offering valuable insights into the importance of transparency, accountability, and responsiveness in management practices. As institutions strive to navigate the complexities of human interactions, the lessons learned from this situation should inform future policies and procedures, ensuring that they are designed to promote fairness and equity.

CHAPTER NINETEEN: JUDGE AND JUROR CONSIDERATIONS

In summary, the case of Taylor and Steen at the MTC/Gary Job Corps Center underscores the critical importance of effective management practices in educational institutions. The documentation of complaints, the necessity of robust rebuttals to unwarranted accusations, and the challenges faced in engaging management in meaningful dialogue all highlight the complexities inherent in organizational governance. As such, it is imperative that institutions prioritize the establishment of clear communication protocols and adhere to their own policies to foster an environment conducive to resolution and growth. The implications of these findings extend beyond the immediate context, serving as a reminder of the need for continuous reflection and improvement in management practices to ensure the well-being of all stakeholders involved.

In examining the conduct of Ms. Benson, it becomes evident that her actions deviated significantly from the standards of professional behavior expected within the workplace. The failure to investigate the concerns raised not only undermines the integrity of the professional environment but also raises questions regarding the legitimacy of her threats to impose disciplinary measures without substantiated evidence. Such actions, devoid of a foundation in factual occurrences, contravene the principles of fairness and transparency that should govern professional interactions.

Furthermore, it is imperative to highlight that the appropriate protocol for addressing grievances should have involved a systematic approach, beginning with the 3-12 shifts RN Supervisor, followed by a comprehensive discussion with the shift staff. This would have ensured that all parties had the opportunity to engage in an open forum, thereby fostering a culture of accountability and mutual respect. The absence of such dialogue not only exacerbates misunderstandings but also perpetuates an atmosphere of mistrust.

Moreover, the assertion that the narrator had no prior knowledge regarding the records in question is crucial to understanding the context of the allegations. It is essential to clarify that they had never experienced sabotage from any non-management co-worker, nor would they ever engage in such unethical behavior. *The commitment to uphold a standard of conduct that is respectful and professional is paramount.* Any deviation from these standards warrants immediate reporting, confrontation, and documentation.

It is also significant to note the timeline of events surrounding the alleged incident. The claim that the issue occurred on October 11, 2004, is factually incorrect, as the incident in question transpired on August 23, 2004, coinciding with the commencement of the narrator's forced transfer to the 3:00 PM to 12:00 midnight shift. The delayed response to this matter, which was only addressed following the meeting with Dr. G and Mr. Pena on October 11, 2004, raises further concerns regarding the handling of the situation.

Lastly, the allegation regarding the narrator's refusal to retrieve medication for Ms. Rosa Ortiz, a Nurse Practitioner, is a misrepresentation of the facts. It is important to assert that Ms. Ortiz had the capacity to procure the medication independently, and the collaborative nature of nursing necessitates prioritizing the needs of students while adhering to professional responsibilities.

Thus, it is imperative to approach these matters with clarity and a commitment to factual accuracy, ensuring that all parties are held accountable for their actions within the professional framework.

In the context of workplace dynamics and interpersonal relationships, the situation involving Mary Beth and her subsequent actions toward the narrator exemplifies a profound misalignment of professional ethics and managerial integrity. Upon her promotion to Health Service Administrator, Mary Beth's decision to exclude the narrator from her team, as communicated to Barbara Garza, raises significant questions regarding her leadership style and the implications of such exclusionary practices within organizational structures.

The incident at Wendy's Fast Food, where Mary Beth's loud demeanor reportedly caused embarrassment to Frank Silbas, further illustrates the potential for unprofessional conduct to permeate workplace interactions, thereby affecting not only individual reputations but also the overall morale of the team. The subsequent actions taken by Mary Beth, including the issuance of write-ups and the unfounded allegations of theft, reflect a troubling pattern of behavior that undermines the principles of fairness and transparency that are essential in any professional environment.

Moreover, the manipulation of facts regarding the narrator's responsibilities, as evidenced by the misrepresentation of duties to senior management and HR, underscores a significant breach of trust. The transition to a Performance Improvement Plan (PIP) based on a backlog of paperwork, which was exacerbated by the withdrawal of assistance from Mr. Pena following Mary Beth's deceitful claims, highlights the detrimental impact of such managerial misconduct on employee performance and well-being. The recommendation for the narrator to move to CPP by senior center management, ostensibly framed as a supportive measure, is perceived as a strategic maneuver to mitigate the fallout from the ongoing conflict rather than a genuine effort to address the underlying issues. *This situation illustrates the complexities of navigating workplace politics, where the fear of retribution can compel individuals to accept unfavorable conditions for the sake of job security.*

The narrative surrounding Mary Beth's actions serves as a cautionary tale about the ramifications of unethical leadership and the importance of fostering a culture of accountability and respect within organizations. The implications of such experiences extend beyond individual grievances, impacting the collective ethos of the workplace and the overall efficacy of organizational operations.

In light of the aforementioned circumstances, it is imperative to underscore the critical importance of safeguarding sensitive information, particularly in the context of personnel and medical records. The assertion that Ms. Smith, despite her purported expertise, failed to adhere to established protocols regarding the handling of such records raises significant concerns about negligence and accountability. The improper removal of sensitive documents, including licenses, without the requisite consent or notification of the responsible custodian not only contravenes ethical standards but also poses a substantial risk of criminal liability, potentially culminating in charges of identity theft or fraud.

Furthermore, the timeline of events surrounding the disappearance of these records warrants meticulous examination. Ms. Steen's last documented entry into the files in late August 2004, juxtaposed with Ms. Smith's departure on September 1, 2004, suggests a critical window during which the files could have been improperly accessed or removed.

This temporal gap accentuates the necessity for a thorough investigation into the chain of custody of these documents, as well as the protocols that govern their management. Moreover, the failure to notify all affected employees or license holders regarding the missing files constitutes a breach of duty that exacerbates the potential for harm.

Such notification is not merely a procedural formality; it is an essential component of ensuring that individuals can take proactive measures to protect their personal information. Consequently, the lack of communication from supervisory personnel in this instance reflects a systemic failure that must be addressed to prevent future occurrences.

The implications of this situation extend beyond individual negligence; they highlight the need for robust policies and practices that prioritize the protection of sensitive information. It is incumbent upon all stakeholders within the organization to recognize their responsibilities in safeguarding such data and to implement measures that ensure compliance with legal and ethical standards.

CHAPTER TWENTY: SPECIFIC ALLEGATIONS AND CONCERNS

In examining the systemic issues surrounding workplace discrimination and the perpetuation of a hostile work environment, it is imperative to consider the multifaceted nature of the allegations presented. The statement by Phyllis Smith, RN, Health Services Administrator, which references derogatory comparisons between black employees and criminality, underscores a troubling trend of racial bias that permeates the organizational culture. Such remarks not only reflect a profound lack of professionalism but also serve to reinforce harmful stereotypes that unjustly associate black individuals with criminal behavior, thereby undermining their autonomy and dignity within the workplace.

Furthermore, the denial of vacation requests to black employees, while similar requests from Caucasian and Hispanic employees were granted, exemplifies a discriminatory practice that is both significant and deeply concerning. This disparity in treatment raises critical questions about the fairness and equity of human resource policies at the Gary Job Corps Center. The subsequent actions taken against a black employee, including the issuance of a Performance Improvement Plan (PIP) following complaints about unrealistic work expectations, further illustrate the retaliatory measures that often accompany such discriminatory practices.

The involvement of Carol Benson, RN, Nursing Supervisor, in fostering a hostile work environment by provoking conflicts and challenging established Job Corps procedures, despite her limited experience, highlights the detrimental impact of leadership that lacks both awareness and sensitivity to the complexities of workplace dynamics. This behavior not only exacerbates tensions among staff but also contributes to an atmosphere of fear and mistrust.

Moreover, the actions of Mary Beth Magovsky, RN, Health Services Administrator, who allegedly engaged in gossip about black employees and subsequently denied such behavior, reflect a broader pattern of undermining the credibility and integrity of black staff members. *The creation of a paper trail to discredit a long-serving employee who has dedicated twelve years to the organization is emblematic of a calculated effort to marginalize voices that challenge the status quo.*

Jury Evidence Review

The allegations presented reveal a pervasive culture of discrimination and hostility that not only affects individual employees but also undermines the overall efficacy and ethical standing of the organization. It is essential for institutions to critically examine their practices and implement comprehensive training programs aimed at fostering inclusivity and respect, thereby ensuring that all employees are treated with the dignity they deserve.

In examining the systemic issues surrounding workplace discrimination and the perpetuation of a hostile work environment, it is imperative to consider the multifaceted nature of the allegations presented. The statement by Phyllis Smith, RN, Health Services Administrator, which references derogatory comparisons between black employees and criminality, underscores a troubling trend of racial bias that permeates the organizational culture. Such remarks not only reflect a profound lack of professionalism but also serve to reinforce harmful stereotypes that unjustly associate black individuals with criminal behavior, thereby undermining their autonomy and dignity within the workplace.

Furthermore, the denial of vacation requests to black employees, while similar requests from Caucasian and Hispanic employees were granted, exemplifies a discriminatory practice that is both significant and deeply concerning. This disparity in treatment raises critical questions about the fairness and equity of human resource policies at the Gary Job Corps Center. The subsequent actions taken against a black employee, including the issuance of a Performance Improvement Plan (PIP) following complaints about unrealistic work expectations, further illustrate the retaliatory measures that often accompany such discriminatory practices.

The involvement of Carol Benson, RN, Nursing Supervisor, in fostering a hostile work environment by provoking conflicts and challenging established Job Corps procedures, despite her limited experience, highlights the detrimental impact of leadership that lacks both awareness and sensitivity to the complexities of workplace dynamics. This behavior not only exacerbates tensions among staff but also contributes to an atmosphere of fear and mistrust.

Moreover, the actions of Mary Beth Magovsky, RN, Health Services Administrator, who allegedly engaged in gossip about black employees and subsequently denied such behavior, reflect a broader pattern of undermining the credibility and integrity of black staff members. *The creation of a paper trail to discredit a long-serving employee who has dedicated twelve years to the organization is emblematic of a calculated effort to marginalize voices that challenge the status quo.*

Additionally, the allegations presented reveal a pervasive culture of discrimination and hostility that not only affects individual employees but also undermines the overall efficacy and ethical standing of the organization. It is essential for institutions to critically examine their practices and implement comprehensive training programs aimed at fostering inclusivity and respect, thereby ensuring that all employees are treated with the dignity they deserve.

Considering these developments, it is crucial to analyze the implications of management's actions and their subsequent impact on employee morale and workplace dynamics. The abrupt alteration of Geraldine Taylor's responsibilities, particularly following the appointment of Ms. Smith as Health Services Administrator, raises significant questions regarding the transparency and fairness of organizational practices. The lack of a clear job description and appropriate training for the newly created position not only undermines the professional development of employees but also reflects a broader systemic issue within the management structure.

Furthermore, Ms. Smith's attempt to coerce Ms. Taylor into participating in actions against a fellow employee, Glenda Steen, highlights a troubling dynamic that fosters an environment of distrust and hostility among staff members. Such behavior not only contravenes ethical standards expected in professional settings but also exacerbates existing grievances, necessitating a more robust framework for addressing employee concerns.

Consequently, the decision to escalate complaints to higher authorities is not merely a reactionary measure but a critical step toward fostering a culture of accountability and respect within the workplace. By formally documenting these grievances, employees assert their rights and advocate for equitable treatment, reinforcing the notion that management must engage constructively with the workforce to cultivate a healthy organizational climate.

The situation described reveals a profound and troubling pattern of systemic discrimination and managerial negligence within the workplace. The assertion that complaints directed to senior management and the main consultant went unaddressed underscores a significant failure in organizational accountability. This lack of response not only exacerbates feelings of incompetence and frustration but also highlights a broader issue of inequity that appears to be rooted in racial bias.

Furthermore, the realignment of personnel, as articulated by Ms. Smith, raises critical questions regarding the motivation behind such decisions. The transition to a new shift, coupled with the assertion that the day shift would consist solely of white nurses, starkly illustrates a potential violation of principles of diversity and inclusion. The juxtaposition of staffing arrangements—whereby the evening shift retains most minority staff—suggests a deliberate segregation that warrants further scrutiny.

The subsequent dismissal of concerns regarding harassment, defamation, and discrimination by both Ms. Smith and Ms. Benson, alongside the inaction from HR and center administration, reflects a troubling culture of impunity. The issuance of a comprehensive 20-page complaint document signifies a desperate attempt to seek redress, yet the absence of any follow-up meetings or investigations indicates a systemic disregard for the grievances of minority employees.

Considering these circumstances, the decision to engage legal counsel becomes not merely a personal recourse but a necessary step in confronting the pervasive issues of racial discrimination and unprofessional conduct that have been systematically ignored. The implications of such a scenario extend beyond individual experience, calling into question the ethical standards and operational integrity of the management at the center. Thus, it is imperative that these matters be addressed with the seriousness they deserve, ensuring that all employees, regardless of their racial or ethnic background, are treated equitably.

In examining the recent developments within the operational framework of the Wellness Center, it is imperative to acknowledge the significant strides made under the narrator's administration, which had previously ensured compliance with the standards set forth by the US Department of Labor. The collaborative environment fostered among staff members, alongside the adherence to established procedures by students, exemplified a well-functioning institution.

However, the abrupt shift toward non-compliance, characterized by numerous violations, raises critical questions regarding the underlying dynamics at play, particularly considering the apparent biases exhibited by Ms. Smith and Ms. Benson toward the narrator's position as a Licensed Vocational Nurse (LVN) rather than a Registered Nurse (RN). It is noteworthy that the Wellness Center has experienced a notable turnover in Health Services Administrators over the past three years, with the narrator's tenure being marked by a commitment to stability and operational excellence despite the challenges posed by frequent leadership changes.

The pattern of complaints initiated by Geraldine, which seemed to trigger a series of retaliatory actions from Ms. Smith and Ms. Benson, suggests a troubling environment where dissent is met with hostility rather than constructive dialogue. This situation culminated in a deliberate attempt to provoke insubordination, thereby creating grounds for potential termination under MTC Policy.

Furthermore, the treatment received by the narrator, particularly in relation to shift assignments and overall job responsibilities, appears to be a calculated effort to undermine their position and compel resignation. In a recent meeting with both Ms. Smith and Ms. Benson, the narrator explicitly communicated an intention to remain steadfast in their role despite the forced alterations to duties and the unwarranted challenges to professional integrity. *It is essential to assert that they will continue to advocate for their rights and address these concerns through all available channels, ensuring that the principles of respect and equity are upheld within the workplace.*

In addressing the concerns raised during the staff meeting, it is imperative to emphasize the fundamental right of employees to express their viewpoints in an open forum. The primary objective of such meetings is to facilitate dialogue regarding pertinent issues, thereby fostering a collaborative environment.

CHAPTER TWENTY-ONE: THE ALLEGATION PART TWO

Regarding the allegation of raising my voice, it is essential to clarify that this action was not intended as an act of insubordination; rather, it was a necessary measure to ensure that my communication was effectively conveyed and comprehended by all present. The assertion that my vocal projection constituted disruptive behavior lacks substantiation, particularly in the absence of a clear explanation from Ms. Benson regarding the nature of the alleged disruption.

Furthermore, the claim of inappropriate conduct is equally unfounded. My opposition was directed solely towards the threats of unwarranted disciplinary action based on unverified accusations made by the Swing Shift RN. The statement, *"If it happens again, I'm going to write you up,"* was met with my firm refusal to accept such unjust treatment. *It is crucial to note that Ms. Benson's failure to investigate these serious allegations undermines the integrity of the complaint process and reflects a lack of adherence to professional standards.*

In light of these circumstances, it is reasonable to assert that the right to address grievances in an open forum is not merely a privilege but an earned right as an employee. Should Ms. Benson wish to implement a structured approach to staff meetings, including parliamentary procedures that delineate when and how staff members may speak, such guidelines must be formally established and communicated to all employees. This would ensure clarity and fairness in the conduct of future meetings, thereby promoting a more respected and equitable workplace environment.

The complexities surrounding workplace dynamics, particularly within institutional frameworks such as the Gary Job Corps Center, necessitate a thorough examination of management practices and their implications on employee welfare. Following a series of over twenty-five documented complaints directed towards the center management, it became increasingly apparent that the existing mechanisms for addressing grievances were insufficient. Consequently, the decision to pursue federal intervention through the Equal Employment Opportunity Commission (EEOC) emerged as a necessary course of action. *This narrative delineates the rationale behind this decision, the specific violations encountered, and the broader implications for employee rights and organizational accountability.*

Context and Significance of the Issue

The Gary Job Corps Center, as a pivotal institution, is aimed at providing vocational training and support to young individuals and is expected to uphold a standard of professionalism and ethical conduct. However, the pervasive issues reported by employees indicate a systemic failure within the management structure. The complaints, which ranged from discriminatory practices to hostile work environments, underscored a profound disconnect between the center's stated mission and the lived experiences of its employees. This dissonance not only jeopardizes the well-being of the workforce but also undermines the efficacy of the center's educational objectives. *Thus, the significance of addressing these grievances extends beyond individual cases; it encompasses the integrity of the institution itself.*

Documentation of Violations

During my research into the EEOC process, meticulous documentation of the violations was undertaken, serving as the foundation for a potential case filing. The violations identified were consistent with the basic standards outlined by the EEOC, which include, but are not limited to, discriminatory treatment based on race, gender, and age, as well as retaliation against employees who voiced concerns. Furthermore, the hostile work environment fostered by certain management members not only contravened established labor laws but also created an atmosphere of fear and intimidation among employees. *Such conditions are antithetical to the principles of autonomy and respect that should govern any workplace, particularly one dedicated to the development of young individuals.*

Management's Response and Employee Impact

The response from the Management and Training Cooperation, as well as the Gary Job Corps Center management, has been characterized by a lack of accountability and transparency. Despite numerous attempts to resolve the issues through internal channels, the absence of meaningful dialogue or corrective action has perpetuated a cycle of discontent. Employees, who are often the most productive members of the organization, have found themselves marginalized and demoralized, leading to a significant decline in morale and productivity. *The implications of such a toxic environment are far-reaching, affecting not only individual employees but also the overall mission of the center to provide effective training and support.*

The Decision to Seek Federal Intervention

Given the gravity of the situation and the ineffectiveness of internal resolution mechanisms, the decision to seek federal intervention through the EEOC was both a strategic and ethical imperative. The EEOC serves as a critical arbiter in matters of workplace discrimination and employee rights, providing a platform for grievances to be addressed at a federal level. *This course of action is not merely a recourse for individual grievances; it represents a collective stand against systemic injustices that have been allowed to fester within the organization.* By pursuing this avenue, the aim is to not only rectify the specific violations encountered but also to instigate a broader cultural shift within the management practices at the Gary Job Corps Center.

In summation, the issues encountered at the Gary Job Corps Center highlight significant deficiencies in management practices that have led to a detrimental work environment for employees. The decision to document these violations and seek federal intervention through the EEOC is a necessary step toward restoring integrity and accountability within the institution. *As the process unfolds, it is imperative to reflect on the broader implications of such actions, not only for the individuals directly affected but also for the organizational culture as a whole.* Ultimately, the pursuit of justice in this context serves as a reminder of the fundamental rights of employees and the ethical obligations of management to foster a respectful and equitable workplace.

CHAPTER TWENTY-TWO: ADVERSE ACTION

It is established by law under Title VII of the Federal Equal Opportunity Act that adverse actions encompass a variety of retaliatory measures that can significantly impact an individual's employment status and professional trajectory.

General Types of Adverse Actions

The most apparent forms of retaliation include denial of promotion, refusal to hire, denial of job benefits, demotion, suspension, and discharge. However, the spectrum of adverse actions extends beyond these overt measures; it also encompasses subtler forms of retaliation such as threats, reprimands, negative evaluations, harassment, or other detrimental treatment. As articulated by the Ninth Circuit, the degree of harm suffered by the individual is pertinent to the issue of damage rather than liability. To establish unlawful retaliation, it is imperative to demonstrate that the respondent undertook an adverse action as a direct consequence of the charging party's engagement in protected activity.

Proof of this retaliatory motive can be substantiated through either direct or circumstantial evidence. The evidentiary framework applicable to other discrimination claims similarly extends to retaliation claims.

Direct Evidence

In instances where credible direct evidence indicates that retaliation was a motivating factor behind the challenged action, a finding of *"cause"* should be established. Evidence pertaining to any legitimate motive for the challenged action is relevant solely to the issue of relief, not to liability. Direct evidence of a retaliatory motive encompasses any written or verbal statement made by a respondent official indicating that the adverse action was taken because the charging party engaged in protected activity. *Such evidence may also include statements that, on their face, reveal a bias against the charging party based on their protected activity, coupled with evidence that links this bias to the adverse action.* A demonstrable connection could be established if the statement was articulated by the decision-maker at the time of the adverse action. It is noteworthy that direct evidence of retaliation is relatively rare.

Circumstantial Evidence

Conversely, circumstantial evidence serves as the most prevalent method for substantiating claims of retaliation. This form of evidence may include a variety of indicators that, when considered collectively, suggest a retaliatory motive. Such indicators may encompass patterns of behavior, temporal proximity between the protected activity and the adverse action, and the presence of similarly situated individuals who were treated more favorably. *The synthesis of these elements can create a compelling narrative that supports the assertion of retaliatory intent, thereby reinforcing the claim of unlawful retaliation under Title VII.*

In closing, the complexities surrounding adverse actions necessitate a nuanced understanding of both direct and circumstantial evidence, particularly within the framework of employment discrimination and retaliation claims. The case presented illustrates how perceptions of qualifications can be influenced by subjective criteria, as evidenced by the assertion that the selectee was better qualified due to her possession of a master's in business administration, while the complainant held only a college degree. This rationale, however, is called into question by the EEOC investigator, who finds that the emphasis on experience, which has historically been the most significant criterion for selection in management positions, undermines the legitimacy of the selectee's qualifications.

Furthermore, the second example highlights the intricate dynamics of retaliation, where the complainant alleges that a negative job reference was issued as a direct consequence of filing an EEOC charge. The evidence presented indicates that the negative statements made to the prospective employer were, in fact, honest assessments of the complainant's job performance, thereby negating any claims of pretext. In contrast, the third example reveals a failure to adhere to established policies regarding the provision of job performance information, suggesting a potential inconsistency that raises questions about the credibility of the employer's explanations.

The concept of temporary or preliminary relief emerges as a critical mechanism for addressing retaliation before it escalates, particularly when there exists a substantial likelihood that the challenged action will be deemed unlawful. While courts have historically ruled that financial hardships do not constitute irreparable harm, it is essential to recognize that the broader implications of job loss—such as emotional distress and reputational damage—may indeed lead to irreparable consequences. *Thus, proven retaliation is often characterized by malice or reckless indifference to federally protected rights, underscoring the need for vigilant oversight and accountability within organizational practices.*

In the realm of healthcare management, adherence to protocols and the meticulous documentation of patient care are paramount, particularly in the context of medication administration. This narrative seeks to elucidate the events surrounding the medication requests made by Delia Allen and Amanda Boatman at the wellness center on October 30, 2005, while also examining the implications of these incidents within the broader framework of compliance and accountability in healthcare settings. *The significance of these occurrences lies not only in the immediate concerns regarding medication management but also in the potential systemic issues that may arise when proper procedures are not followed.*

Documentation and Communication Failures

The initial incident involving Delia Allen raises critical questions regarding the adequacy of communication and documentation practices within the wellness center. On the aforementioned date, Allen reported to the facility requesting her medication, specifically spironolactone (Aldactone) 25mg, which she claimed to have received a few days prior. However, a review of her medical chart reveals a conspicuous absence of documentation detailing the quantity of medication dispensed or the rationale for its prescription. This lack of clarity is compounded by the fact that all recorded blood pressure readings for Allen were within normal limits, thereby prompting inquiries into the necessity of the medication itself.

Furthermore, the prescribing physician, Dr. Hood, provided a note for the student to retain, yet there is no evidence to suggest that the medication was ordered or that any follow-up inquiries were made to ascertain the appropriateness of the treatment. *Such oversights not only undermine the integrity of patient care but also raise concerns about the potential for medication errors, which could have significant ramifications for patient health and safety.*

Subsequent Medication Request and Implications

On the same day, Amanda Boatman also approached the wellness center to collect her medication. While the specifics of her case are not detailed in the documentation, the parallel nature of these incidents underscores a potential pattern of inadequate medication management practices within the facility. The juxtaposition of these two cases highlights the necessity for robust systems of checks and balances to ensure that all medication requests are handled with the utmost diligence and care. The implications of these incidents extend beyond individual patient experience; they reflect broader systemic issues that may be present within the wellness center's operational framework.

The absence of clear protocols for medication management, coupled with insufficient documentation practices, can lead to a cascade of errors that jeopardize patient safety and violate established healthcare regulations. Consequently, these failures necessitate a thorough investigation and a reevaluation of existing policies to prevent recurrence. The events surrounding the medication requests made by Delia Allen and Amanda Boatman on October 30, 2005, serve as a poignant reminder of the critical importance of effective communication, thorough documentation, and adherence to established protocols within healthcare settings. *The potential ramifications of these incidents underscore the necessity for healthcare providers to prioritize patient safety and compliance with regulatory standards.* As such, it is imperative that the wellness center undertake a comprehensive review of its medication management practices to ensure that similar issues do not arise in the future, thereby safeguarding the well-being of its patients and upholding the integrity of the healthcare system.

Management Failures and Systemic Issues

In examining the ongoing issues surrounding the behavior of Ms. Smith and Ms. Benson, it becomes increasingly apparent that a systematic failure exists within the management structure, particularly at the senior level. The lack of intervention from corporate management, despite numerous complaints and concerns articulated in both verbal and written formats, suggests a troubling pattern of negligence that undermines the integrity of the institution. This absence of accountability not only perpetuates a toxic environment but also raises significant ethical questions regarding the protection of students' legal rights, which appear to have been disregarded.

Furthermore, the poignant reflections of Parks, who demonstrated remarkable courage in the face of adversity, serve as a stark reminder of the ongoing struggle against discrimination. *As articulated by Senate Chaplain Barry Black, Parks' actions ignited a movement that awakened the national conscience, highlighting the profound impact of seemingly small acts of defiance.* This historical context underscores the necessity for continued vigilance in the fight against racial inequality, which remains pervasive in various facets of society, including educational institutions.

Consequently, it is imperative that Black Americans, and indeed all individuals committed to social justice, dedicate themselves wholeheartedly to combating the insidious nature of discrimination that persists in South Texas and beyond. The deeply ingrained biases that influence interpersonal interactions, educational practices, and employment opportunities must be confronted with unwavering resolve. *As we reflect on the progress made thus far, it is crucial to acknowledge that the journey toward true equality is far from complete; rather, it is a continuous endeavor that demands both collective action and individual commitment.*

This was my true and raw anger and emotions at the time of these horrible actions. It's never-ending with written complaints to management.

Vacation Requests and Discriminatory Practices

In the context of the events described, it is imperative to analyze the implications of systemic issues within the workplace, particularly concerning the dynamics of power and discrimination. The memorandum of conversation, dated July 1, 2004, highlights a troubling scenario wherein Ms. Steen and the narrator faced significant obstacles in securing their vacation requests, ostensibly due to the actions of Ms. Smith, who was perceived as exhibiting discriminatory behavior.

The initial encounter with Human Resources, involving Melissa Valdez and Barbara Coe, underscores a dismissive attitude towards the grievances expressed by the two employees. Their laughter in response to the serious allegations of racial bias not only trivializes the concerns raised but also reflects a broader culture of insensitivity that can permeate organizational structures. *This reaction is particularly concerning as it suggests a lack of accountability and a failure to address the underlying issues of racism that may be affecting workplace morale and employee well-being.*

Furthermore, the subsequent communication with Mr. Pena reveals a critical moment where the narrator attempts to articulate the pervasive nature of Ms. Smith's alleged discriminatory practices. The mention of previous incidents involving Hispanic employees, such as Ms. Aranda and Anita Zamora, serves to contextualize the narrator's claims within a pattern of behavior that raises significant ethical questions regarding Ms. Smith's conduct. The assertion that Ms. Smith's actions have led to the departure of multiple employees due to harassment not only strengthens the case for a thorough investigation but also highlights the detrimental impact of such behavior on the organizational culture.

The events surrounding the vacation requests and the interactions with Human Resources illuminate the urgent need for a comprehensive examination of workplace policies and practices. *It is essential for organizations to foster an environment that prioritizes inclusivity and addresses any form of discrimination, thereby ensuring that all employees are treated with the dignity and respect they deserve.* The implications of these discussions extend beyond individual grievances, calling for systemic change that promotes equity and accountability within the workplace.

I am personally tired of her bringing my name into her negative conversations. It seems that anything with a negative connotation, she mentions my name. I am hoping I will not have to take these issues to another level.

Staff Complaints and Ethical Misconduct

The complexities surrounding workplace dynamics, particularly within healthcare settings, often reveal underlying issues of discrimination, harassment, and ethical misconduct. The case involving the complaints lodged against certain staff members at a healthcare center underscores the profound implications of such grievances, not only for the individuals directly involved but also for the institutional integrity and operational efficacy of the organization.

This narrative aims to elucidate the significant concerns raised by Diana Rios, a Nursing Supervisor, regarding Mary Beth Magovsky, the Health Services Administrator, while also addressing the broader context of ongoing complaints and the implications of documented misconduct by Melissa Valdez, the Human Resources Manager. The persistent complaints that have emerged from the center's staff reflect a troubling atmosphere characterized by fear and mistrust. As reported, these grievances have escalated, with some originating from individuals who previously participated in attempts to discriminate against colleagues such as Geraldine and Glenda Steen. *This pattern of behavior suggests a systemic issue within the organizational culture, where certain staff members feel emboldened to engage in discriminatory practices without fear of repercussion.*

The ramifications of such actions extend beyond individual experiences, potentially fostering an environment that undermines the principles of equity and respect that are essential in healthcare settings.

CHAPTER TWENTY-THREE: SPECIFIC ALLEGATIONS AND CONCERNS

Diana Rios's request for a confidential meeting with Human Resources Specialist Claudia A. Pastrano underscores the urgent need to address specific concerns regarding Mary Beth Magovsky. Ms. Rios articulated feelings of discomfort, which may indicate a broader pattern of unprofessional conduct or a hostile work environment perpetuated by Ms. Magovsky. The implications of such discomfort are significant, as they can lead to decreased morale, increased turnover, and, ultimately, a decline in the quality of care provided to patients. Furthermore, the reluctance of staff to report grievances due to fear of retaliation exacerbates the issue, creating a cycle of silence that allows misconduct to persist unchecked.

Documentation of Misconduct

The case of Melissa Valdez, who has been accused of providing false testimony during a deposition, serves as a critical example of the potential consequences of unethical behavior within human resources. Despite her denial of reported incidents, records indicate that her actions were well-documented, raising questions about her credibility and the integrity of the human resources department. The failure to hold Ms. Valdez accountable for her alleged perjury not only undermines trust in the human resources function but also sends a troubling message to staff regarding the seriousness with which complaints are taken.

Such a lack of accountability can perpetuate a culture of impunity, where individuals feel justified in engaging in unethical behavior without fear of consequences.

Implications for Organizational Integrity

The ongoing issues at the center, particularly the complaints against both Mary Beth Magovsky and Melissa Valdez, highlight the critical need for organizations to foster a culture of transparency and accountability. Failure to address complaints adequately can lead to a toxic work environment, ultimately impacting patient care and organizational reputation. Furthermore, the implications of these grievances extend beyond the immediate context, as they may influence the broader discourse surrounding workplace ethics and the responsibilities of human resources in safeguarding employee rights.

In summary, the complaints raised by Diana Rios regarding Mary Beth Magovsky, coupled with the documented misconduct of Melissa Valdez, illuminate the pressing need for organizations to prioritize ethical conduct and accountability. The ramifications of failing to address such issues are profound, affecting not only the individuals involved but also the overall integrity of the institution. As organizations navigate the complexities of workplace dynamics, it is imperative that they cultivate an environment where grievances can be reported without fear of retaliation, ensuring that all employees are treated with the dignity and respect they deserve.

The ongoing situation at the center serves as a poignant reminder of the critical importance of ethical leadership and the necessity of fostering a culture of transparency and accountability in the workplace.

Regarding this Information

In the context of the ongoing discourse surrounding workplace dynamics, it is imperative to address the allegations presented in the correspondence dated September 9, 2005, which outlines significant staff complaints against the individual in question. The complaints, articulated by Mrs. Geraldine Taylor, Ms. Nobia Cockrum, and Ms. Diana Rios, highlight a troubling pattern of alleged harassment, discrimination, and unprofessional conduct that has purportedly fostered a hostile work environment.

The allegations assert that Mrs. Taylor has experienced ongoing hostility, which she attributes directly to the actions of the accused, thereby suggesting a detrimental impact on her professional well-being. Similarly, Ms. Cockrum's claims of unprofessional conduct further underscore the need for a thorough examination of interpersonal relations within the workplace.

Ms. Rios's assertion that her ability to perform her duties as a Nurse Supervisor has been compromised due to an uncomfortable work environment adds another layer of complexity to the situation, indicating that the ramifications of such behavior extend beyond individual grievances to affect overall team functionality.

In light of these serious allegations, the recommendations provided, which include fostering effective communication and engaging in team-building exercises, are not merely procedural but rather essential steps toward restoring a collaborative and respectful workplace culture. The suggestion to attend Leadership Training by October 31, 2005, serves as a proactive measure aimed at equipping the individual with the necessary skills to navigate interpersonal challenges and mitigate future conflicts. Furthermore, the emphasis on notifying supervisory personnel for assistance when addressing staff concerns reflects a commitment to transparency and accountability, which are crucial in maintaining a professional environment.

It is vital to recognize that the organization's stance on prohibiting unacceptable behavior is not only a matter of policy but also a fundamental aspect of ethical leadership.

The bottom line is that the resolution of this matter, while deemed satisfactory by the administration, necessitates ongoing vigilance to ensure that the principles of respect, autonomy, and professionalism are upheld within the workplace. The implications of these allegations extend beyond the immediate context, serving as a reminder of the profound impact that leadership behavior can have on staff morale and organizational integrity.

In the context of the complex dynamics within the healthcare setting described, it is imperative to analyze the implications of the assignments and interactions among staff members, particularly in relation to Ms. Taylor and Ms. Cooper. The decision to assign Ms. Taylor to the triage/care unit, contingent upon the volume of students requiring attention, reflects a strategic approach to resource allocation; however, it also raises questions regarding the equitable distribution of responsibilities among staff.

The delineation of roles, wherein Ms. Cooper is relegated to the care unit, ostensibly to minimize her exposure to regular triage duties, suggests an underlying tension that merits further examination.

Moreover, the behavior exhibited by Ms. Abel, who consistently reminded the author of the number of students awaiting care despite the author's engagement in charting, underscores a potential bias in the treatment of staff based on race. This observation is particularly salient when juxtaposed with the segregationist practices purportedly endorsed by Mary Beth Magovsky, who allegedly facilitated a division of labor along racial lines, thereby perpetuating systemic inequities within the clinic. The reference to a "hit list" compiled by certain staff members to undermine the author's position is indicative of a hostile work environment, one that is exacerbated by the existing power dynamics and racial tensions.

Furthermore, the actions taken by Mary Beth Magovsky, particularly in light of the pending appeals related to a previous lawsuit and the current EEOC filing, illustrate a calculated effort to maintain control over the narrative surrounding the author's employment status. The absence of signatures from the corporate office on the termination documents, as presented by Magovsky, raises significant concerns regarding the legitimacy of the termination process and the adherence to proper protocols.

All in all, the intricate interplay of personal and professional relationships within this healthcare environment not only reflects broader societal issues of race and power but also highlights the urgent need for systemic reform to ensure that all staff members are treated with fairness and respect, free from discrimination and retaliation.

On January 19, 2006, Geraldine contacted Mario Sandoval to inform him of the author vacating the premises. Following this, she relayed the information to Melissa Valdez, emphasizing the necessity of retrieving the security deposit. Consequently, the author proceeded to Human Resources on January 20, 2006, as per Melissa's instructions. However, the secretary, Connie Montgomery, informed the author that the request had not been processed.

The situation escalated on January 23, 2006, when the author reached out to Mario Sandoval regarding the status of the deposit, particularly in light of Melissa's prior assurance that it would be available by Friday. In a perplexing turn of events, Mario asserted, "She does not have anything to do with housing," which contradicted Melissa's earlier indication that all matters concerning the situation were to be directed through her. This inconsistency raised significant concerns regarding the clarity of communication within the Human Resources department.

Furthermore, on January 19, 2005, Patricia Luna informed the author that Lois Cooper had expressed a willingness to comply with any directives from Mary Beth Magovsky, ostensibly to secure her employment. This revelation underscores a troubling dynamic within the workplace, where job security appears to influence the integrity of communications and decisions made by staff members.

It is noteworthy that several individuals who were similarly dismissed reported being directed to Human Resources without prior appointments, suggesting a systemic issue within the organization. Following the author's application for unemployment benefits, an investigation concluded that the termination was deemed unjust by the employer. This determination has significant implications for the author's eligibility for benefits, reflecting a broader pattern of employment practices that warrant scrutiny.

On Tuesday, August 23, 2005, Nobia Cockrum, LVN, approached Barbara Coe in the Human Resources department to discuss her experiences and perceived mistreatment within the Wellness Center. During their conversation, Ms. Cockrum recounted an earlier meeting with Ms. Rios, the Nurse Supervisor, which had been prompted by a complaint lodged by Ms. Gaines, LVN. Ms. Rios informed Ms. Cockrum that Ms. Gaines had expressed dissatisfaction regarding the lack of assistance she received from both Ms. Cockrum and Ms. Taylor.

In response, Ms. Cockrum asserted that Ms. Cooper, the designated float nurse, should have been the one to provide support to Ms. Gaines. Furthermore, Ms. Cockrum articulated her frustration to Ms. Rios, indicating that if Ms. Gaines were to spend less time outside smoking, she might be more capable of managing her caseload effectively. Ms. Cockrum also highlighted a recurring issue: whenever she found herself overwhelmed with work, she received no assistance from the supervisory staff. This led her to express feelings of discrimination within the department, a sentiment she elaborated upon during her discussion with Ms. Rios.

In a specific instance, Ms. Cockrum noted that only she and Ms. Taylor were responsible for performing pap smears, a situation that arose after Ms. Gaines complained about an unpleasant odor in the medication room. Ms. Cockrum conveyed to Ms. Rios that both she and Ms. Magovsky harbored distrust towards Ms. Cockrum and Ms. Taylor in the medication room, which further exacerbated the tensions within the team.

Additionally, Ms. Cockrum recounted an incident where Ms. Magovsky requested assistance in the medication room after Ms. Elizondo left without completing her duties. Despite Ms. Cooper's complaints regarding her own discomfort, Ms. Cockrum pointed out the inequity in the distribution of responsibilities, emphasizing that all staff members experienced similar physical challenges yet were not afforded the same considerations.

This ongoing situation, characterized by perceived inequities and a lack of support, underscores the broader issues Barbara Coe elucidates regarding the intricate dynamics within the organizational framework of Gary Job Corps. Each individual's contributions construct a nuanced understanding of the policies and procedures shaping the Plaintiff's professional experiences.

Consequently, it becomes evident that the interplay of these various perspectives is not merely additive but creates a comprehensive tapestry elucidating the complexities inherent in the Plaintiff's employment history. This detailed examination reveals the critical importance of equitable treatment among nursing staff. By understanding the multifaceted interactions and their impact on individual and collective performance, it becomes clear that fostering an inclusive and fair workplace is essential.

Equitable treatment not only enhances the morale and productivity of the nursing staff but also ensures a cohesive and supportive work environment that benefits both employees and the organization. Through this lens, the call for policies and practices that promote fairness and respect within the workplace is underscored.

The experiences at Gary Job Corps highlight the need for ongoing evaluation and adjustment of organizational procedures to safeguard the well-being and professional growth of all staff members. This commitment to equity is foundational to building a workplace culture that values and leverages the diverse strengths and perspectives of its team.

Furthermore, it is essential to recognize that the insights provided by these key figures are not isolated; they are interwoven with the institutional ethos of Gary Job Corps, which emphasizes both the autonomy of its employees and the overarching regulatory environment governing their roles. This synthesis of knowledge aids in clarifying the Plaintiff's trajectory while inviting a broader discourse on the implications of employment practices within such organizations.

To bring it all together, the collaborative efforts of these knowledgeable individuals underscore the profound significance of the Plaintiff's employment history while reflecting the intricate web of policies and interpersonal relationships that define the operational landscape of Gary Job Corps. This analysis enriches our understanding of the Plaintiff's experiences while serving as a critical reminder of the importance of contextualizing individual narratives within the larger institutional framework.

CHAPTER TWENTY-THREE: FIRST CASE FILING

In the realm of workplace dynamics, the complexities surrounding issues of discrimination and harassment often necessitate a multifaceted approach to resolution. The case of Geraldine and Glenda Steen serves as a poignant illustration of the challenges faced by employees ensnared in a web of systemic injustice. Their story dissects the myriad dimensions of their experience, elucidating the procedural intricacies and emotional ramifications that accompany such predicaments. By examining their journey, insights can be gained into the broader implications of workplace discrimination and the essential steps needed to foster a more equitable environment.

To fully appreciate the gravity of the situation faced by Geraldine and Glenda, it is imperative to contextualize their experiences within the broader framework of workplace discrimination. Discrimination in the workplace can manifest in various forms, including but not limited to gender bias, racial prejudice, and retaliation against whistleblowers. Each form of discrimination can create a hostile work environment that not only affects the targeted individuals but also impacts overall workplace morale and productivity.

The psychological toll of enduring such treatment can be profound, often leading to diminished job performance, increased anxiety, and a pervasive sense of helplessness. In this particular instance, the Steens were confronted with a series of egregious behaviors that not only undermined their professional integrity but also threatened their emotional well-being. Their experiences highlight the urgent need for organizations to implement robust policies and training programs aimed at preventing discrimination and fostering inclusivity.

Initially, Geraldine and Glenda attempted to address their grievances through the established channels of center management. This approach, while commendable in its intent, often proved to be fraught with obstacles. The reluctance of management to acknowledge the severity of the issues at hand is a common phenomenon in many organizational structures, where the preservation of the status quo often takes precedence over the pursuit of justice. This reluctance can stem from a variety of factors, including fear of legal repercussions, concerns about public image, or a lack of understanding regarding the implications of discriminatory behavior. Consequently, the Steens found themselves in a protracted cycle of complaints that yielded little in the way of substantive resolution. This experience is not unique; many employees face similar challenges when attempting to voice their concerns, leading to a culture of silence that further perpetuates discrimination.

The Decision to Seek Outside Intervention

As the situation deteriorated, it became increasingly evident to Geraldine and Glenda that their plight required intervention beyond the confines of internal management. The decision to pursue external avenues for resolution is often laden with apprehension, particularly in environments where retaliation is a palpable threat. In this case, the Steens were acutely aware of the potential repercussions that could arise from escalating their concerns.

The fear of retaliation can be a significant deterrent for many employees, leading them to question whether their pursuit of justice is worth the potential personal and professional costs. Nevertheless, the imperative to seek justice ultimately outweighed their fears, prompting them to explore alternative strategies. This decision marked a critical turning point in their journey, as it signified their determination to reclaim their rights and seek accountability for the injustices they faced.

In navigating the labyrinthine landscape of employment law, the significance of meticulous documentation cannot be overstated. Building a prima facie case necessitates a comprehensive record of events, including dates, times, and specific instances of discriminatory behavior. This process requires not only diligence but also a keen analytical eye to synthesize the information into a coherent narrative that underscores the severity of the situation.

Throughout this phase, I provided guidance to the Steens, emphasizing the necessity of maintaining an exhaustive account of their experiences. *This documentation would serve as the bedrock of their case, bolstering their claims with concrete evidence.* Furthermore, having a well-documented account can empower individuals by providing them with a sense of control over their narrative, allowing them to articulate their experiences with clarity and confidence.

The emotional ramifications of enduring workplace discrimination are often profound and far-reaching. Geraldine and Glenda, like many individuals in similar circumstances, experienced heightened levels of stress and anxiety as they grappled with the uncertainty of their situation. The psychological burden of feeling marginalized and unsupported can lead to a pervasive sense of isolation, further exacerbating the challenges they faced.

It is crucial to acknowledge that the emotional toll of such experiences can be as damaging as the discriminatory actions themselves, necessitating a holistic approach to resolution that addresses both the legal and psychological dimensions of the issue. Support systems, such as counseling services and peer support groups, can play a vital role in helping individuals process their experiences and develop coping strategies to navigate the emotional landscape of workplace discrimination.

CHAPTER TWENTY-FOUR: ENGAGEMENT WITH EXTERNAL RESOURCES

Considering the challenges encountered with center management, the Steens were encouraged to engage with external resources specializing in workplace discrimination. These organizations often provide invaluable support, offering legal advice, counseling services, and advocacy on behalf of affected employees. The decision to seek assistance from such entities represents a pivotal moment in the journey toward justice, as it empowers individuals to reclaim their autonomy and assert their rights in the face of adversity.

Furthermore, the involvement of external advocates can amplify the voices of those who have been marginalized, fostering a sense of solidarity among individuals facing similar challenges. By connecting with others who have navigated comparable experiences, the Steens could find reassurance and validation, reinforcing their resolve to pursue justice.

Legal Considerations and the Role of Attorneys

While the Steens initially operated without legal representation, the complexities of employment law necessitate a thorough understanding of the legal landscape. Engaging an attorney who specializes in employment discrimination can provide critical insights into the nuances of the law, as well as the potential avenues for recourse available to the Steens. An attorney can assist in navigating the intricacies of filing a formal complaint, ensuring that all procedural requirements are met and that the case is presented in a compelling manner.

The absence of legal counsel at this stage posed a significant risk, as the intricacies of the law can often be daunting for individuals without formal training. Moreover, having legal representation can lend credibility to the claims being made, as attorneys can articulate the legal implications of the Steens' experiences in a manner that resonates with decision-makers.

Management's Response and Accountability

Throughout this process, it is essential to consider the role of management in perpetuating or alleviating the issues at hand. The numerous notices provided to Gary Management regarding the Steens' grievances underscore a critical aspect of organizational accountability. The failure to address these concerns in a timely and effective manner not only reflects poorness in management but also raises questions about the ethical standards upheld within the organization.

The reluctance to engage with the Steens' complaints can be interpreted as a tacit endorsement of the discriminatory behaviors they endured, thereby perpetuating a toxic workplace culture. This lack of accountability can have far-reaching consequences, not only for the individuals directly affected but also for the overall organizational climate, as it can foster an environment where discrimination is tolerated and unchallenged.

Reflecting on the Implications

The case of Geraldine and Glenda Steen serves as a microcosm of the broader challenges faced by individuals confronting workplace discrimination. The journey from initial complaints to the decision to seek external intervention is fraught with emotional turmoil, procedural complexities, and the ever-present threat of retaliation.

As they navigate this labyrinthine process, the importance of documentation, legal representation, and external support becomes increasingly evident. Ultimately, the implications of their struggle extend beyond their individual experiences, shedding light on the systemic issues that pervade many organizational structures. It is incumbent upon society to foster environments that prioritize equity and justice, ensuring that the voices of those who have been marginalized are heard and validated.

Through a concerted effort to address these issues, it is possible to cultivate workplaces that not only uphold the principles of autonomy and dignity but also serve as bastions of support for all employees. By learning from individuals like the Steens, organizations can take proactive steps to create a culture of inclusivity and respect, ultimately benefiting both employees and the organization.

In the aftermath of the disheartening conversation with Pittard, whose demeanor was marked by an unsettling distance and a lack of empathy, the profound implications of his actions—or, rather, his inactions—became clear. The reliance on a mere letter to communicate critical developments regarding the case, rather than a personal phone call, epitomized a troubling disregard for the emotional weight borne by clients in such precarious situations. *This lack of compassion was particularly disconcerting, given Pittard's purported commitment to civil rights advocacy.*

Subsequently, a visit to Glenda's office offered a glimmer of solace. Prior to arriving, Geraldine had been contacted, only to relay that administrative duties prevented her from meeting at that moment. Standing before Glenda's office, the sight of Geraldine traversing the administrative corridor became a poignant reminder of the emotional toll this ordeal had exacted on all involved. The expression of sheer pain etched on her face resonated deeply, mirroring the anguish apparent in Glenda's countenance.

At that moment, overwhelmed by the weight of shared struggles, seeking comfort in Glenda's embrace while yearning to extend support to Geraldine felt inevitable.

The arduous journey undertaken in pursuit of justice was not lost on Glenda and Geraldine. They were acutely aware of the countless hours dedicated to meticulously crafting and refining documentation in anticipation of potential court proceedings. The thought of relinquishing this fight was inconceivable, particularly in light of the suffering endured by loved ones and friends, inflicted by those in positions of power who exhibited a blatant disregard for their responsibilities.

Re-engagement with the task at hand became imperative, fueled by an unwavering commitment to advocating for their rights.

Thus, Pattard was contacted once more, with an insistence on the necessity of obtaining all relevant case files. Surprisingly, he acquiesced swiftly, even offering to deliver the materials to San Marcos. The meeting at the Outlet Mall stood out vividly, where a substantial box filled with critical legal documents was handed over. At that moment, an inquiry was made about the possibility of an appeal; however, Pittard's evasive response, coupled with his admission of a new job, left a sense of foreboding regarding the prospects for justice.

In contemporary society, workplace discrimination remains a pervasive issue, particularly affecting marginalized groups. The statistics presented in the 2002 Rutgers University study, *A Workplace Divided: How Americans View Discrimination and Race on the Job*, revealed a stark contrast in the experiences of African American workers compared to their white counterparts. This story explores the multifaceted dimensions of workplace discrimination, its psychological ramifications, and the broader implications for society. By delving deeper into these aspects, a better understanding can be gained of the complexities of discrimination and the urgent need for change.

Understanding Workplace Discrimination

Workplace discrimination is defined as the unfair treatment of individuals based on characteristics such as race, gender, age, or sexual orientation. The Rutgers study highlighted that 46 percent of African American workers believed they had been subjected to unfair treatment by their employers, a figure that starkly contrasted with the mere 10 percent of white workers who reported similar experiences. This disparity underscored the systemic nature of discrimination, often rooted in historical and socio-economic contexts.

Discrimination manifested in various forms, including overt actions such as harassment and subtle biases influencing hiring and promotion decisions. Understanding these nuances remained crucial for addressing the issue effectively.

Statistical Insights Into Discrimination

The statistics provided by the Rutgers study were not only alarming but also indicative of a broader societal issue. The findings revealed that 28 percent of African Americans and 22 percent of Hispanics/Latinos experienced workplace discrimination, compared to only 6 percent of whites. These figures suggested that minority groups were disproportionately affected by discriminatory practices, which often included hiring biases, unequal pay, and limited opportunities for advancement.

Furthermore, the impact of these discriminatory practices extended beyond the workplace, affecting the economic stability and social mobility of entire communities. The systemic nature of these issues called for a comprehensive approach to dismantling the barriers perpetuating inequality.

The Burden Of Proof

As Murrell articulated, the burden of proof often fell on workers who believed they were being discriminated against. This expectation led to significant psychological distress, as individuals grappled with self-doubt and a lack of confidence in their professional capabilities.

The necessity to prove discrimination created an environment where employees felt compelled to endure unfair treatment rather than risk their employment status by voicing their concerns. *This dynamic perpetuates a culture of silence,* discouraging individuals from seeking help or reporting incidents, further entrenching discriminatory practices within organizations.

Psychological Ramifications Of Discrimination

The psychological impact of workplace discrimination extended beyond the confines of the office; feelings of hopelessness, mistrust, despair, and alienation often permeate an individual's life, affecting their interactions with family and friends.

Why does it feel like this never ends? The stress and depression arising from such experiences often led to withdrawal from social engagements, exacerbating feelings of isolation. This cycle of emotional turmoil had profound implications on an individual's overall well-being, often leading to long-term mental health issues.

Research showed that individuals who experienced workplace discrimination were at a higher risk for anxiety disorders, depression, and even physical health problems, illustrating the far-reaching consequences of such experiences.

Impact On Family Dynamics

Discrimination did not merely affect the individual; it also had a ripple effect on family dynamics. When an employee experienced unfair treatment at work, the resultant stress often spilled over into their home life, impacting relationships with partners, children, and extended family members.

How can they even understand this weight? The emotional burden carried by the affected individual often led to increased tension and conflict within the household, as family members struggled to understand the source of their loved one's distress.

Moreover, children might internalize their parents' struggles, leading to issues in their own social interactions and academic performance. This intergenerational impact highlighted the need for addressing workplace discrimination not only for the sake of individual employees but also for the health and stability of families and communities.

Consequences for Organizational Culture

Organizations that failed to address workplace discrimination harmed not only individual employees but also jeopardized their overall organizational culture. A workplace characterized by discrimination often led to decreased morale, reduced productivity, and higher turnover rates.

Furthermore, the reputational damage incurred by organizations perceived as discriminatory had long-lasting effects on their ability to attract and retain talent. Employees who felt valued and respected were more likely to be engaged and committed to their work, while those who experienced discrimination disengaged, leading to a toxic work environment.

This underscored the importance of fostering a culture of inclusivity and respect within organizations.

Legal Framework And Protections

In response to the pervasive issue of workplace discrimination, various legal frameworks were established to protect employees.

The Civil Rights Act of 1964, for instance, prohibited employment discrimination based on race, color, religion, sex, or national origin. However, despite these legal protections, many individuals remained unaware of their rights or felt intimidated by the prospect of pursuing legal action against their employers.

This gap between legal protection and employee awareness underscored the need for comprehensive education and advocacy efforts. Organizations must not only comply with legal standards but also actively promote awareness of these rights among their employees, ensuring everyone understood the protections available to them.

Strategies for Addressing Discrimination

To combat workplace discrimination effectively, organizations must implement proactive strategies fostering an inclusive environment. These could include diversity training programs, establishing clear anti-discrimination policies, and promoting open dialogue regarding issues of bias and inequality.

Furthermore, organizations should create safe channels for employees to report discrimination without fear of retaliation, empowering individuals to advocate for their rights. Regular assessments of workplace culture and employee feedback could help organizations identify areas for improvement and measure the effectiveness of their initiatives.

By prioritizing inclusivity, organizations could create a more equitable workplace that benefited everyone.

CHAPTER TWENTY-FIVE: THE ROLE OF LEADERSHIP IN PROMOTING EQUITY

Leadership plays a crucial role in shaping organizational culture and addressing discrimination. Leaders must not only endorse anti-discrimination policies but also model inclusive behavior and hold themselves accountable for fostering a diverse workplace. By prioritizing equity and inclusion, they can create an environment where all employees feel valued and respected, mitigating the negative impacts of discrimination.

Additionally, leaders should actively seek diverse perspectives in decision-making processes, ensuring that the voices of marginalized groups are heard and considered. *This commitment to equity at the leadership level sets a powerful example for the entire organization.*

The Path Forward

Workplace discrimination remains a significant issue affecting a substantial portion of the workforce, particularly among marginalized groups. The findings from the Rutgers University study illuminated the stark realities faced by African American and Hispanic/Latino workers, highlighting the urgent need for systemic change.

Addressing workplace discrimination requires a multifaceted approach encompassing legal protections, organizational strategies, and a commitment to fostering an inclusive culture. By acknowledging the profound psychological ramifications of discrimination and implementing effective measures to combat it, society can move toward a more equitable future where all individuals are afforded the dignity and respect they deserve in their professional lives.

The journey toward equity is ongoing. Vigilance and proactive efforts are imperative to creating a fair and just workplace for everyone.

Harassment in the Workplace

- National Origin
- Pregnancy
- Race/Color
- Religion
- Retaliation
- Sex
- Sexual Harassment

Harassment, as delineated by various legal frameworks, constitutes a significant violation of employee rights, manifesting in myriad forms that undermine the integrity of the workplace. It is imperative to recognize that harassment is not merely an isolated incident but rather a pattern of behavior that creates a hostile or offensive environment, infringing upon the autonomy and dignity of the affected individual.

The legal definitions encompass a wide array of discriminatory practices, including slurs, derogatory comments, and unwelcome sexual advances, all contributing to an atmosphere of intimidation and fear. Furthermore, the implications of harassment extend beyond immediate interactions, often resulting in severe adverse employment decisions such as demotion or termination.

The harasser may occupy various roles within the organizational hierarchy, from supervisors to coworkers or even external parties such as clients, complicating the dynamics of accountability and responsibility.

In addition, the McDonnell Douglas test serves as a critical framework for assessing claims of discrimination. This test establishes a structured approach to determine whether a prima facie case exists. It necessitates a thorough examination of the claimant's status as a member of a protected class, their qualifications for the position, and the circumstances surrounding the alleged discriminatory actions.

By synthesizing these elements, one can ascertain the validity of claims and the extent to which the workplace environment has been compromised. Consequently, organizations must implement robust policies and training programs to prevent harassment and foster an inclusive workplace culture. Such measures not only protect employees but also enhance overall organizational efficacy by promoting a climate of respect and collaboration.

The legal and ethical ramifications of harassment underscore the necessity for vigilance and proactive engagement in addressing these critical issues within the realm of employment.

Navigating Claims of Discrimination

No single piece of evidence is typically sufficient to substantiate claims of discrimination. Instead, the complexity of such cases often necessitates a multifaceted approach to evidence-gathering. Conversely, there exists no definitive "magic" quantity or type of evidence required to establish a case of discrimination.

In instances where an employer is reluctant to acknowledge its transgressions or rectify underlying issues, it may become imperative for the aggrieved party to escalate their concerns to the Equal Employment Opportunity Commission (EEOC) or the relevant state fair employment agency.

The apprehension is real. Employees often experience trepidation when contemplating the disclosure of discriminatory practices within their workplace. This fear frequently arises from the possibility of retaliation or jeopardizing their livelihoods. As a result, many individuals choose to overlook, evade, or disregard such injustices, perceiving this as the safer alternative.

Various tools and methodologies can facilitate the documentation necessary for pursuing legal action. The narrative presented in *Dark Hearts Iron Hands* serves as a vital resource, empowering individuals to advocate for justice within their workplaces. Discriminatory practices must never be condoned or tolerated; instead, they should be actively challenged and dismantled.

When confronted with the urgent need to address these pressing issues, it became apparent that many individuals were reluctant to engage in dialogue. Some actively attempted to dissuade the efforts, their discontent palpable. Murmurs of dissent and, at times, overtly negative responses from those around were undeniable.

It was evident that, for an extended period, certain acquaintances — referred to as "frenemies" — expressed disapproval vocally, suggesting that the case should not be pursued. *Their reluctance was steeped in a fear of failure,* reflecting the pervasive culture of silence that often surrounds issues of discrimination.

CHAPTER TWENTY-SIX: PERPETUATING A CYCLE OF SILENCE AND COMPLICITY

In contemporary society, workplace discrimination remains a pervasive and insidious problem affecting countless individuals across various sectors. This story seeks to explore the multifaceted nature of workplace discrimination, focusing on the legal frameworks that exist to protect employees, the societal implications of racism, and the historical context that has shaped current attitudes and practices. By examining these elements in detail, a nuanced understanding of the challenges faced by employees in combating discrimination is developed. The exploration of workplace discrimination is essential not only for understanding the current landscape but also for envisioning a future where equity and justice prevail in professional environments.

Workplace discrimination is defined as the unfair treatment of employees based on certain characteristics, including but not limited to race, gender, age, disability, and sexual orientation. This discrimination manifests in various forms, including hiring practices, promotions, job assignments, and terminations. It also extends to harassment and hostile work environments, where individuals face derogatory comments or actions that undermine their dignity and professional standing.

The legal landscape surrounding workplace discrimination is complex, with numerous laws and regulations designed to protect employees from such injustices. However, despite these protections, many employees remain unaware of their rights and the mechanisms available to challenge discriminatory practices. *This lack of awareness often leads to a culture of silence,* where individuals suffer in isolation rather than seeking the support and recourse they deserve.

In the United States, several key pieces of legislation provide a framework for addressing workplace discrimination. The Civil Rights Act of 1964, particularly Title VII, prohibits employment discrimination based on race, color, religion, sex, or national origin. Additionally, the Americans with Disabilities Act (ADA) of 1990 protects individuals with disabilities from discrimination in the workplace. The Age Discrimination in Employment Act (ADEA) of 1967 further safeguards older workers from age-based discrimination.

These laws establish a legal basis for employees to file complaints against discriminatory practices. However, the process of proving such acts can be daunting and often requires a thorough understanding of legal standards. To successfully prove a case of discrimination, employees must typically demonstrate that they belong to a protected class, experienced adverse employment action, and that there is a causal connection between their protected status and the adverse action.

This legal requirement is largely unknown or ignored by many employees, leading to significant underreporting of discriminatory incidents. Furthermore, the fear of retaliation often discourages individuals from coming forward, perpetuating a cycle of silence and complicity within organizations. This fear is compounded by the reality that many employees rely on their jobs for financial stability, making the prospect of challenging their employer particularly daunting.

Racism, as a form of workplace discrimination, not only harms individuals but also has profound implications for society as a whole. *The normalization of racist attitudes and behaviors creates a toxic work environment,* leading to decreased morale, productivity, and overall job satisfaction. Moreover, the systemic nature of racism means that its effects extend beyond the workplace, influencing broader societal dynamics and perpetuating inequality.

The ramifications of workplace racism contribute to economic disparities, as marginalized groups often find themselves systematically excluded from opportunities for advancement and fair compensation. Racism is dismissive and represents an ignorant approach to human interaction. The historical context of racism, particularly in the United States, reveals a legacy of oppression that has shaped contemporary attitudes.

During the early years of slavery, for instance, Black individuals were dehumanized and regarded as property rather than human beings. *This devaluation of Black lives has had lasting repercussions,* contributing to a culture in which racial discrimination is often overlooked or dismissed. The societal acceptance of such attitudes leads to a cycle of discrimination that is difficult to break, as new generations inherit these biases and perpetuate them in various forms.

Organizations play a critical role in either perpetuating or combating workplace discrimination. Many companies have implemented diversity and inclusion initiatives aimed at fostering a more equitable work environment. These initiatives often include training programs, mentorship opportunities, and policies designed to promote diversity at all levels of the organization.

However, the effectiveness of these initiatives hinges on the genuine commitment of leadership to address systemic issues.

Unfortunately, some organizations have largely ignored the problem of discrimination, employing heavy-handed tactics to challenge those who dare to voice their concerns. This approach undermines trust between employees and management, perpetuating a culture of fear that stifles open dialogue about discrimination.

Moreover, organizations must recognize that diversity initiatives should not be mere checkboxes to fulfill compliance requirements. *Real change demands genuine effort,* where equity and inclusion are embedded into the organizational fabric rather than treated as superficial measures.

Instead, diversity and inclusion initiatives should be integrated into the core values and mission of the organization, ensuring that all employees feel valued and respected. This requires ongoing assessment and adaptation of policies to meet the evolving needs of a diverse workforce.

Education and awareness are crucial components in the fight against workplace discrimination. Employees must be informed about their rights and the legal protections available to them. Furthermore, organizations should prioritize training programs that educate employees about the various forms of discrimination and the importance of fostering an inclusive workplace.

By promoting awareness and understanding, organizations can empower employees to recognize and challenge discriminatory behaviors without fear of retaliation. Educational initiatives should extend beyond compliance training to include discussions about the impact of unconscious bias and the importance of allyship in the workplace. *Creating a culture of awareness leads to more proactive measures against discrimination,* as employees become equipped with the knowledge and tools necessary to advocate for themselves and their colleagues.

Historical Context: The Legacy of Slavery and Its Impact on Modern Discrimination

The historical legacy of slavery in the United States serves as a critical backdrop for understanding contemporary issues of racism and discrimination. The dehumanization of Black individuals during slavery, coupled with the subsequent Jim Crow laws and systemic racism, created a societal framework in which racial discrimination continues to thrive.

The scars of this history are evident in the ongoing disparities in employment, education, and economic opportunities faced by marginalized communities. Furthermore, the historical narrative surrounding racism often overlooks the resilience and agency of those who have fought against oppression.

The civil rights movement, for instance, exemplifies the collective efforts of individuals who challenged discriminatory practices and sought to dismantle systemic racism. *This historical context underscores the importance of recognizing the ongoing struggle for equality and justice in the workplace.* By understanding this legacy, organizations can better appreciate the significance of their role in fostering an inclusive environment and addressing the lingering effects of discrimination.

Reflecting On The Implications Of Discrimination

Workplace discrimination remains a significant issue that requires urgent attention and action. The legal frameworks designed to protect employees from discrimination are often underutilized, and the societal implications of racism continue to reverberate throughout various sectors.

Organizations must take proactive steps to address discrimination and foster an inclusive work environment, while employees must be empowered to understand their rights and challenge discriminatory practices. Ultimately, the fight against workplace discrimination is not merely a legal obligation but a moral imperative that demands collective action and commitment to creating a more equitable society.

As progress continues, it is essential to recognize that the journey toward equality is ongoing. By fostering open dialogue, promoting education, and holding organizations accountable, the structures of discrimination can be dismantled, paving the way for a future where every individual is valued and respected in the workplace.

The commitment to equity must be unwavering, as it reflects not only our values but also a crucial step toward *redefining societal dynamics.* The civil rights movement illuminated pervasive injustices faced by marginalized communities while underscoring the necessity of reevaluating the values underpinning collective existence.

The movement, while catalyzing significant legislative changes, often found itself ensnared in paradoxes where institutions designed to uphold justice became arenas of further oppression. *This duality is exemplified in experiences at the Gary Job Corps Center,* where systemic neglect of individual grievances reflected a broader societal malaise.

In this context, the assertion that *"black lives should matter to black lives"* serves as a poignant reminder of internalized struggles that must be addressed before external accountability can be effectively pursued. Autonomy within the community is paramount; it is through the establishment of self-worth and mutual respect that a foundation for broader societal change is constructed.

The experiences of Geraldine and Glenda illustrate the detrimental effects of institutional apathy, where the voices of those who have dedicated their lives to service are rendered insignificant in the face of bureaucratic indifference. Furthermore, the dissonance between personal accolades and professional recognition raises critical questions about the criteria by which competence is assessed within institutions.

The reliance on character references from colleagues, juxtaposed with the dismissal of their testimonies, reveals a troubling trend where systemic biases overshadow individual merit. *This phenomenon perpetuates cycles of disenfranchisement,* highlighting the urgent need for reform within organizational structures that claim to champion equality.

Consequently, it is imperative that the lessons gleaned from these narratives inform ongoing discourse surrounding civil rights and social justice. By fostering an environment where the value of every individual is recognized and upheld, society can begin dismantling the oppressive frameworks that have historically marginalized voices.

In doing so, not only are the sacrifices of those who came before honored, but a more equitable future is paved—one where the principles of justice and dignity are universally applied.

CHAPTER TWENTY-SEVEN: CRAFTING CASE PROCEEDINGS

The correspondence presented in the document serves as a significant artifact encapsulating the essence of organizational communication within a corporate framework, particularly in the context of management training and development. The letter, addressed to Geraldine Taylor from the Senior Vice President of Management Training Corporation, conveys appreciation for the efforts made at the Gary Job Corps Center while reflecting broader themes of institutional improvement, employee recognition, and the cultivation of a model community. The story aims to dissect various elements of the letter, exploring its implications and the underlying principles governing effective communication in professional settings.

To fully appreciate the nuances of the letter, it is essential to establish the context in which it was written. The Gary Job Corps Center is a facility that provides vocational training and educational opportunities to young individuals, often from disadvantaged backgrounds. This center plays a crucial role in bridging the gap between education and employment, offering programs that equip participants with the skills necessary to thrive in the workforce. The Wellness Center, a component of this institution, plays a pivotal role in ensuring the holistic development of its participants, addressing not only their educational needs but also their physical and emotional well-being.

The date of the letter, November 14, 2001, situates it within a specific historical moment marked by significant shifts in educational policy and workforce development strategies in the United States. During this period, there was a growing recognition of the importance of vocational training as a means to combat unemployment and poverty, particularly among youth. The emphasis on improving living and learning conditions within such centers reflects a broader societal commitment to enhancing the quality of life for marginalized populations. This context underscores the importance of the initiatives being undertaken at the Gary Job Corps Center and the role of effective communication in promoting these efforts.

One of the most salient features of the letter is its focus on recognition and appreciation. The Senior Vice President of Management Training Corporation (MTC) explicitly commends Geraldine for her hard work and dedication, which are crucial elements in motivating employees and enhancing job satisfaction.

The structure of the letter, presented as evidence to the court, is formal yet approachable, characteristic of professional correspondence. It begins with a clear salutation, addressing Geraldine Taylor directly, and establishing a personal connection. The opening lines express gratitude for the opportunity to visit the Wellness Center, setting a positive tone maintained throughout the communication. This initial acknowledgment serves as both a courtesy and a strategic move to foster goodwill and encourage continued collaboration. The structure of the letter, with its clear organization and logical flow, enhances its effectiveness as a communication tool, allowing the recipient to easily grasp the key messages being conveyed.

Moreover, the use of concise paragraphs and straightforward language contributes to the letter's clarity. Each paragraph addresses a specific theme, making it easier for Geraldine to identify the main points of recognition and appreciation. This thoughtful organization reflects an understanding of the recipient's perspective and the importance of delivering messages in a manner that is both respectful and engaging.

It should be noted that research in organizational behavior suggests recognition significantly impacts employee morale and productivity. Thus, acknowledging individual contributions is not merely a formality but a vital component of effective management practices. The letter highlights the improvements made at the Wellness Center, suggesting these advancements result from the collective efforts of the staff, reinforcing the notion of teamwork and shared responsibility.

This emphasis on recognition extends beyond mere acknowledgment; it serves as a powerful motivator for continued excellence. By celebrating individual achievements, the organization cultivates an environment where employees feel valued and inspired to contribute their best efforts. This practice enhances individual performance and fosters a culture of collaboration and mutual support among team members, ultimately benefiting the organization.

The tone of the letter reflects an organizational culture that values transparency, communication, and employee engagement. By publicly recognizing the contributions of individuals like Geraldine, the Senior Vice President reinforces a culture of appreciation that can lead to enhanced loyalty and commitment among employees. This practice aligns with contemporary theories of organizational development, advocating for inclusive environments where employees feel valued and empowered to contribute to the organization's mission. The letter, therefore, serves as a microcosm of the broader cultural dynamics at play within Management Training Corporation.

Additionally, the letter's emphasis on open communication fosters a sense of belonging among employees. When individuals feel their contributions are acknowledged and appreciated, they are more likely to engage actively in their roles and collaborate with their colleagues. This sense of belonging is crucial for building a cohesive team that works towards common goals, ultimately enhancing the organization's overall effectiveness.

In addition to its implications for organizational culture, the letter speaks to the broader theme of community development. The reference to making Gary a "model living and learning community" underscores the organization's commitment to not only improving the facilities but also fostering an environment conducive to personal and professional growth. This vision aligns with principles of community engagement and social responsibility, increasingly recognized as essential components of successful educational and training programs. By investing in the development of such communities, organizations can contribute to the empowerment of individuals and the betterment of society.

The commitment to community development is further exemplified by the initiatives undertaken at the Gary Job Corps Center, which aim to create a supportive environment for young individuals. These initiatives provide vocational training and promote life skills, mentorship, and personal development, ensuring participants are well-equipped to navigate the challenges of adulthood. The letter serves as a testament to the organization's dedication to fostering a positive impact on both individual lives and the broader community.

The letter addressed to Geraldine Taylor serves as a compelling example of effective communication within a corporate context. It encapsulates key themes of recognition, appreciation, and community development, all integral to fostering a positive organizational culture. The implications of such communication extend beyond the immediate context, influencing employee morale, community engagement, and the overall success of the institution. As organizations navigate the complexities of workforce development and community engagement, the principles exemplified in this correspondence remain relevant, highlighting the enduring significance of effective communication in achieving organizational goals.

Ultimately, the letter reflects the values and priorities of Management Training Corporation while serving as a model for other organizations seeking to enhance their communication strategies. By prioritizing recognition and fostering a culture of appreciation, organizations create an environment where employees feel motivated and empowered to contribute to their fullest potential. In doing so, they not only achieve their organizational objectives but also play a vital role in shaping a more equitable and supportive society.

Barbara Coe, Human Resources Specialist

Cause #MTC000787, statement of fact entered into evidence for court preparations

In contemporary society, the persistent issues surrounding race relations remain a significant concern, revealing a complex interplay of systemic biases and individual behaviors that often go unnoticed. Despite advancements in various domains, the subtle manifestations of racial discrimination continue to permeate social and professional environments. According to the guidelines established by the Equal Employment Opportunity Commission (EEOC), race discrimination encompasses the unfavorable treatment of individuals based on their race or personal characteristics associated with race, such as hair texture, skin color, or specific facial features. Furthermore, color discrimination specifically pertains to the adverse treatment of individuals due to their skin color or complexion, highlighting the nuanced nature of racial biases that can exist even within the same racial group.

Moreover, it is crucial to recognize that race and color discrimination can extend beyond direct interactions, affecting individuals who are associated with or married to people of a particular race or color, as well as those connected to race-based organizations. This broader understanding of discrimination underscores the pervasive nature of racial biases, which manifest in various forms, including workplace environments where individuals may experience discrimination from peers or management, regardless of their own racial identity. The EEOC's comprehensive definitions of race and color discrimination serve to illuminate the unacceptable behaviors prohibited by law, encompassing all aspects of employment, including hiring, firing, pay, job assignments, promotions, layoffs, training, and fringe benefits.

Furthermore, addressing harassment is imperative. Harassment is defined as unlawful behavior directed at individuals based on their race or color. Such harassment may include racial slurs, derogatory remarks, or the display of racially offensive symbols, all contributing to a hostile work environment. While the law does not prohibit simple teasing, any form of harassment creating an intimidating or offensive atmosphere is unacceptable and detrimental to the well-being of individuals affected by such actions.

The ongoing discourse surrounding race relations necessitates a critical examination of both overt and covert forms of discrimination, alongside a commitment to fostering an inclusive environment that respects the dignity and autonomy of all individuals, irrespective of their racial or ethnic backgrounds.

The Dark Hearts believe that through the fusion of man and machine, they can achieve a form of immortality, allowing them to serve the emperor more effectively. This relentless pursuit of perfection drives them to seek out and incorporate the most advanced technologies available, often at the expense of their own humanity.

The Dark Hearts are distinguished not only by their beliefs but also by their appearance and organization. Clad in dark, imposing armor that reflects their somber philosophy, they bear insignia of mechanical parts and skulls, symbolizing their reverence for machinery and the inevitability of death. Their ranks are filled with warriors who have undergone extensive bionic modifications, showcasing their commitment to the machine. In battle, they are known for ruthless efficiency and tactical prowess, employing a combination of heavy firepower and mechanized units to overwhelm their foes.

Within the broader context of the Warhammer 40,000 narrative, Dark Hearts serve as a poignant reminder of the consequences of extreme ideology. Their belief in the superiority of the machine leads to sacrifices other chapters might consider unthinkable, creating a complex dynamic within the Imperium. This reflects the ongoing struggle between humanity and technology, a central theme in the Warhammer 40,000 universe that resonates with fans and players alike.

In Chapter 14 of *Iron Hands,* titled *The Dark Heart,* the story takes a dramatic turn as the Iron Hands face their greatest challenge yet. The chapter delves into the sinister machinations of their enemies and explores the inner turmoil of the Iron Hands as they confront fears and weaknesses. As the plot thickens, key characters are pushed to their limits, revealing unexpected alliances and betrayals. The tension escalates, setting the stage for a climactic showdown testing the resolve and unity of the Iron Hands. This chapter is pivotal, full of suspense and emotional depth as the characters grapple with dark forces threatening their world.

The origins, beliefs, and characteristics of the Iron Hands not only define their identity but also enrich the Warhammer 40,000 lore. Their story exemplifies human ingenuity while serving as a cautionary tale of losing sight of humanity in the relentless pursuit of perfection. This duality makes their narrative compelling and thought-provoking, adding depth to the rich tapestry of the Warhammer universe.

Depositions: Legal proceedings where a party deposes another party or a third person by asking questions under penalties of perjury. The written transcription prepared by the court reporter or notary is called the deposition transcript, not the deposition itself.

Direct Evidence: Evidence based on direct facts, as opposed to circumstantial evidence, which relies on inferences. Direct evidence is believed by reasonable people without needing to draw conclusions. It consists of indisputable facts not requiring any stretch of imagination.

CM/ECF LIVES–U.S. District Court: TX. wd–Docket Report Page 2 of (210)277-362. We needed to present more evidence of the claims made by Geraldine and introduced to the court the information relating to another employee's knowledge that would sway the court.

A Statement Entered Into The Record By Geraldine Regarding Her Co-Worker:

Dorothy Embrey is aware of the problems I have encountered, starting with Phyllis Smith, Carol Benson, and Mary Beth. Mary Beth informed Geraldine that she had seventeen pages of documentation that she would support (what Taylor and Steen said was true). These are the same seventeen pages Mary Beth informed me she had in her possession and would use, asking me to have my previous attorney subpoena her. Dorothy has worked with Geraldine for over seven years and knows her character and work ethic. She can also verify how medications are supposed to be handled as nurses and can confirm the policy or information we were given regarding the removal of records from the Health Services if called to testify in court.

CHAPTER TWENTY-EIGHT: JUDICIAL PROCEEDINGS

In the realm of judicial proceedings, the role of the jury is paramount, serving as the bedrock of the legal system in many jurisdictions. The jury's function is not merely to render a verdict but to engage in a complex process of deliberation that requires a nuanced understanding of both the law and the facts presented during the trial. This discussion aims to elucidate the intricacies of the jury charge, should the case have gone to trial, focusing on the general instructions provided to jurors, the significance of their role as factfinders, and the implications of their verdict. By dissecting these components, the profound responsibility that jurors bear in the pursuit of justice becomes evident.

Understanding the Jury Charge

The jury charge represents a critical juncture in the trial process, wherein the presiding judge articulates the legal standards that the jury must apply to the facts they have heard. This instruction is not merely a formality; it is a vital component shaping the jury's understanding of their duties and the legal framework within which they must operate.

The judge's role is to clarify the law, ensuring that jurors comprehend the principles governing their deliberations. It is essential to recognize that the jury charge is not an expression of the judge's opinion regarding the case's facts; rather, it serves as a guide to the legal standards applicable to the evidence presented.

Moreover, the jury charge often includes specific definitions of legal terms that may be unfamiliar to jurors. Terms such as *reasonable doubt* or *preponderance of the evidence* are defined in a manner that demystifies the legal jargon, allowing jurors to grasp the concepts guiding their decision-making process. This clarity is crucial, as it empowers jurors to engage meaningfully with the evidence and apply the law accurately. The judge may also provide hypothetical scenarios to illustrate how the law applies to the facts, further enhancing jurors' understanding of their responsibilities.

The Role of Jurors

As members of the jury, individuals are entrusted with the solemn responsibility of evaluating the evidence and rendering a verdict based on their findings. This duty necessitates a careful and impartial assessment of the facts, free from any preconceived notions or biases. The jury is tasked with answering specific questions that arise from the evidence, and their responses must reflect a consensus among all jurors, emphasizing the necessity of a unanimous verdict.

This requirement underscores the importance of collaboration and dialogue among jurors, as they must engage in thorough discussions to arrive at a collective conclusion. Furthermore, jurors must be aware of the emotional weight that their decisions carry. The individuals involved in the trial — whether they are victims, defendants, or witnesses — are often deeply affected by the outcome.

Jurors are not just evaluating abstract legal principles; they are making decisions that can alter lives. This understanding adds a layer of gravity to their duty, compelling jurors to approach their task with empathy and a sense of moral obligation. The deliberation process, therefore, becomes not only a legal exercise but also a profound ethical undertaking.

Applying Legal Standards

In the context of the jury charge, the judge delineates various legal standards that jurors must apply to the facts of the case. These standards may include the burden of proof, which typically rests on the prosecution in criminal cases, requiring them to establish the defendant's guilt beyond a reasonable doubt. Conversely, in civil cases, the burden may shift to the plaintiff, who must demonstrate their claims by a preponderance of the evidence.

Understanding these distinctions is crucial for jurors, as they directly influence the weight and interpretation of the evidence presented during the trial. Additionally, jurors must consider the credibility of witnesses and the reliability of the evidence. The jury charge may instruct jurors on how to evaluate witness testimony, including factors such as demeanor, consistency, and potential biases. This aspect of the jury's duty is particularly important, as the quality of evidence can vary significantly, and jurors must discern what is credible and what may be misleading.

The ability to critically assess evidence is a skill that jurors develop through their discussions, and it is essential for reaching a fair and just verdict. Following the jury charge, attorneys for both parties will present their closing arguments. These arguments serve as a synthesis of the evidence and a persuasive appeal to the jury, aiming to reinforce their respective positions. However, it is imperative for jurors to recognize that these statements do not constitute evidence; rather, they are interpretations and arguments intended to elucidate the facts.

Jurors must remain vigilant, focusing on the evidence itself rather than the rhetorical flourishes of the attorneys. This distinction is vital, as it ensures that the jury's decision is grounded in the factual record rather than influenced by persuasive oratory. Moreover, closing arguments often highlight the emotional aspects of the case, appealing to jurors' sympathies and moral judgments. While this can be a powerful tool for attorneys, jurors must be cautious not to let emotions cloud their judgment.

The jury charge serves as a reminder to jurors to remain anchored in the evidence and the law, ensuring that their verdict is based on rational deliberation rather than emotional response. This balance between emotion and reason is a hallmark of the jury's deliberative process.

Unanimous Verdict: A Pillar of Justice

The requirement for a unanimous verdict is a cornerstone of the jury system, reflecting the principle that justice is best served when all jurors agree on the outcome of a case. This unanimity fosters a sense of collective responsibility and accountability among jurors, compelling them to engage in meaningful deliberation and to consider diverse perspectives.

The process of reaching a unanimous decision can be arduous, often necessitating extensive discussions and debates among jurors. However, this deliberative process is essential for ensuring that the verdict reflects a comprehensive evaluation of the evidence and the law. In cases where jurors struggle to reach a consensus, the dynamics of group decision-making come into play. Jurors may experience pressure to conform to the majority opinion, which can lead to a phenomenon known as groupthink.

To counteract this, it is crucial for jurors to foster an environment where dissenting opinions are valued and explored. The jury charge may encourage jurors to voice their concerns and engage in respectful debate, reinforcing the idea that a thorough examination of differing viewpoints ultimately strengthens the integrity of the verdict.

Implications of the Verdict

The implications of the jury's verdict extend far beyond the confines of the courtroom. A guilty verdict can result in significant consequences for the defendant, including potential incarceration, while an acquittal may restore the defendant's freedom and reputation. Furthermore, the jury's decision can have broader societal implications, influencing public perceptions of justice and the legal system. Consequently, jurors must approach their responsibilities with the utmost seriousness, recognizing that their verdict carries weighty consequences for all parties involved.

Additionally, the jury's verdict can set precedents that affect future cases and legal interpretations. In high-profile cases, the public's reaction to the verdict can lead to discussions about systemic issues within the legal system, such as racial bias or the treatment of certain crimes. Jurors, therefore, must be cognizant of the broader context in which their decision is made, understanding that their role extends beyond the immediate case to encompass larger societal implications. This awareness can enhance their commitment to delivering a fair and just verdict.

The Weight of Responsibility

The jury charge serves as a fundamental component of the judicial process, guiding jurors in their deliberations and ensuring that they apply the law correctly to the facts at hand. The duty of the jury is both profound and complex, requiring careful consideration of evidence, a commitment to impartiality, and a dedication to reaching a unanimous verdict. As the arbiters of fact, jurors play a crucial role in upholding the principles of justice, and their decisions resonate far beyond the courtroom.

Thus, it is imperative that jurors approach their responsibilities with diligence and integrity, fully aware of the significant impact their verdicts can have on individuals and society. Ultimately, the jury system embodies the democratic ideals of participation and accountability, allowing ordinary citizens to engage in the administration of justice.

This unique aspect of the legal system not only empowers jurors but also reinforces the notion that justice is a collective endeavor. As such, the jury's role is not just a duty; it is a privilege that carries with it the weight of responsibility to ensure that justice is served fairly and equitably for all.

CHAPTER TWENTY-NINE: CASE PRECEDENCE

The examination of employment discrimination claims, particularly those involving race, necessitates a comprehensive understanding of the legal frameworks established under Title VII of the Civil Rights Act of 1964 and 42 U.S.C. §1981. These statutes serve as pivotal instruments in protecting employees against discriminatory practices in the workplace. This discussion endeavors to elucidate the intricacies of a case involving the termination of a plaintiff on the grounds of alleged race discrimination, focusing on the legal standards and evidentiary requirements that govern such claims. By delving deeper into the nuances of these laws, their significance in promoting workplace equality and justice becomes clearer.

Overview of Title VII and 42 U.S.C. §1981

Title VII prohibits employment discrimination based on race, color, religion, sex, or national origin. It is essential to recognize that this statute not only addresses discriminatory hiring practices but also encompasses various adverse employment actions, including termination, demotion, and harassment. The law applies to employers with 15 or more employees, ensuring that a significant portion of the workforce is protected under its provisions.

Similarly, 42 U.S.C. §1981 provides a federal remedy against racial discrimination in the making and enforcement of contracts, which includes employment contracts. This statute is particularly important as it allows individuals to seek redress in federal court without first exhausting administrative remedies, often required under Title VII. The intersection of these two legal provisions creates a robust framework for addressing grievances related to race discrimination in the workplace, empowering employees to challenge unfair practices and seek justice.

The Concept of Protected Activity

In the context of employment discrimination, the term *protected activity* refers to actions taken by an employee to oppose discriminatory practices or to participate in investigations related to such practices. Title VII protected activities include, but are not limited to, opposing unlawful employment practices, filing a charge of discrimination, and participating in any manner in an investigation or hearing conducted under Title VII.

This concept extends to informal complaints made to supervisors or human resources, as well as formal grievances filed with the Equal Employment Opportunity Commission (EEOC). The significance of this concept cannot be overstated, as it forms the basis for claims of retaliation that may arise following an employee's engagement in such activities. Employees must feel secure in their ability to report discrimination without fear of retribution, making the understanding of protected activities crucial for fostering a fair workplace environment.

The Burden of Proof in Discrimination Claims

When a plaintiff alleges that they were terminated due to their opposition to perceived race discrimination, they bear the burden of proving that they had a reasonable belief that the employment practice in question was unlawful under Title VII.

This standard is critical, as it establishes the threshold for determining whether the plaintiff's actions constitute protected activity. The reasonable belief standard does not require the plaintiff to demonstrate that the discriminatory practice was, in fact, unlawful; rather, it necessitates a showing that the plaintiff held a sincere and reasonable belief that the practice was discriminatory.

This aspect of the law acknowledges that employees may not always have a complete understanding of the legal intricacies surrounding discrimination but still deserve protection when they act on their convictions. The courts often look at the context of the employee's belief, including the nature of the discriminatory behavior and the employee's prior experiences, to assess the validity of their claims.

The Role of Employer's Justifications

In cases where a plaintiff claims retaliation for engaging in protected activity, the employer is permitted to provide justification for the adverse employment action taken against the plaintiff. It is crucial to note that the plaintiff does not need to prove that the unlawful retaliation was the sole reason for their termination.

Instead, if the plaintiff can demonstrate that the employer's stated reasons for termination are disbelieved or found to be pretextual, the jury may infer that the termination was, in fact, motivated by the plaintiff's engagement in protected activity. This means that employers must be prepared to substantiate their claims with credible evidence, such as performance reviews or documented disciplinary actions.

The scrutiny of these justifications often reveals systemic issues within the organization, highlighting the need for employers to maintain transparent and fair practices to avoid potential legal repercussions.

Evaluating the Evidence: The Jury's Role

The jury plays a pivotal role in evaluating the evidence presented in discrimination cases. They are tasked with determining the credibility of the witnesses, the weight of the evidence, and the motivations behind the employer's actions. This process requires jurors to sift through often complex and emotionally charged testimonies, making their role both challenging and critical.

If the jury finds that the reasons provided by the defendant for the termination are not credible, they may conclude that the termination was retaliatory in nature. This underscores the importance of presenting a compelling narrative that highlights inconsistencies in the employer's justification for the adverse action.

Jurors must also consider the broader context of workplace culture and the potential impact of systemic discrimination, which can influence their understanding of the case and the motivations of the parties involved.

Damages and Remedies Available to the Plaintiff

Should the plaintiff successfully prove their claim against the defendant, they may be entitled to various forms of damages. These can include compensatory damages for lost wages, emotional distress, and punitive damages designed to deter the employer from engaging in similar discriminatory practices in the future.

Compensatory damages aim to make the plaintiff whole, covering not only lost income but also expenses related to job searching and potential relocation. Emotional distress damages recognize the psychological toll that discrimination can take on an individual, acknowledging the pain and suffering caused by such experiences.

The determination of damages is often influenced by the severity of discrimination, the impact on the plaintiff's life, and the employer's conduct during the proceedings. In some cases, courts may also order reinstatement or front pay, ensuring that the plaintiff is not left without recourse following a wrongful termination.

Implications for Employment Law

The examination of race discrimination claims under Title VII and 42 U.S.C. §1981 reveals the complexities inherent in proving such cases. The interplay between protected activities, the burden of proof, and the employer's justifications creates a nuanced landscape that requires careful navigation.

As society continues to grapple with issues of race and equality in the workplace, the legal frameworks established by these statutes remain vital in safeguarding the rights of employees. The implications of these cases extend beyond individual claims, influencing broader discussions about workplace equity and the responsibilities of employers in fostering inclusive environments.

Furthermore, the outcomes of these cases can set important precedents that shape future interpretations of employment law, impacting how similar cases are handled in the courts.

In summary, the legal principles surrounding race discrimination and retaliation are critical to understanding the dynamics of employment law. The ability of plaintiffs to articulate their experiences and challenge discriminatory practices is essential in promoting a fair and just workplace. As such, ongoing education and awareness of these legal standards are imperative for both employees and employers alike, ensuring that the tenets of equality and justice are upheld in all employment contexts.

By fostering an environment where employees feel empowered to speak out against discrimination, organizations can not only comply with legal requirements but also contribute to a more equitable society.

Reflecting on the Jury's Deliberation

In the jury's deliberation, it is imperative to reflect on the broader implications of the proceedings and the emotional landscape that enveloped all participants. The culmination of this trial not only signifies the conclusion of a significant legal battle but also serves as a poignant reminder of the complexities inherent in the pursuit of justice.

As the legal team reconvened to dissect the case, it became evident that the atmosphere was charged with a mixture of anxiety and determination. Each member, despite their individual perspectives, shared a common understanding of the arduous journey that had led them to this moment. The weight of the evidence presented, coupled with the emotional investment in the outcome, fostered a sense of camaraderie among the team, even as doubts lingered in the air.

Moreover, the anticipation of the jury's verdict underscored the precarious nature of legal proceedings, where the outcome often hinges on the subjective interpretations of the evidence by jurors. This uncertainty, while unsettling, also galvanized a resolve to continue the fight for justice, regardless of the impending verdict.

The notion that persistence is a valuable commodity resonates deeply within the legal profession, where the stakes are invariably high, and the pursuit of truth can often feel Sisyphean.

Strategic Foresight and Resilience

In contemplating the potential for future actions, such as the filing of additional EEOC complaints, it is crucial to recognize the strategic foresight that accompanies such decisions. Preparedness in the face of adversity not only exemplifies a proactive approach but also reflects an unwavering commitment to advocating for one's rights.

The readiness to escalate the matter further, should the jury's decision prove unfavorable, illustrates a profound understanding of the legal landscape and the necessity of resilience in the face of challenges.

Ultimately, the conclusion of the trial marks not merely an end but rather a transition into a new phase of advocacy and potential legal recourse. The lessons learned throughout this process, coupled with the emotional and intellectual investments made, will undoubtedly inform future endeavors.

As the dust settles on this chapter, it is essential to remain vigilant and prepared for the next steps in the ongoing quest for justice, ensuring that the efforts expended thus far are not rendered moot by a singular outcome.

CHAPTER THIRTY: SUMMARY JUDGEMENT

In the realm of legal disputes, receiving a letter from an attorney, particularly one that conveys the dismissal of a case through Summary Judgment, can be profoundly disorienting and emotionally taxing. This story endeavors to dissect the multifaceted implications of such a scenario, drawing upon personal experiences and broader legal principles to elucidate the complexities inherent in the judicial process. The narrative unfolds with the initial shock of the letter, progresses through subsequent interactions with legal counsel, and culminates in an analysis of the systemic challenges faced by litigants in navigating the intricacies of the legal system. By exploring these dimensions, the emotional and practical ramifications of legal proceedings, along with the importance of effective representation, become clearer.

Initial Reaction to the Summary Judgment Notification

The moment an individual receives a notification regarding a Summary Judgment can be likened to the jarring experience of an unexpected seismic event; it disrupts the status quo and instigates a cascade of emotional responses. Initially, there is a profound sense of disbelief, as the implications of such a judgment are often not immediately comprehensible. The realization that a court has determined, without the necessity of a trial, that there are no genuine disputes of material fact can evoke feelings of vulnerability and helplessness. This emotional turmoil is compounded by the inherent complexities of legal jargon that permeates the notification, rendering it difficult for a layperson to fully grasp the ramifications of the judgment.

As the initial shock subsides, a wave of anxiety often takes its place. Questions flood the recipient's mind: *What does this mean for my case? What are my options now?* The uncertainty can be paralyzing, leading to sleepless nights and an overwhelming sense of dread about the future.

This emotional rollercoaster is not merely a personal experience; it reflects a broader human response to perceived injustice and loss of control over one's circumstances.

Summary Judgment: Legal Principles and Context

To contextualize the emotional response elicited by the Summary Judgment notification, it is imperative to delve into the legal principles underpinning this judicial mechanism. Summary Judgment serves as a procedural device that allows courts to resolve cases without the need for a full trial when there is no genuine issue of material fact. According to the Federal Rules of Civil Procedure, Rule 56, a party may move for Summary Judgment at any time until 30 days after the close of all discoveries.

This rule is predicated on the notion that the judicial system should not be burdened with cases that lack sufficient factual disputes warranting a trial, thereby promoting judicial efficiency. However, the application of Summary Judgment is not without its controversies. Critics argue that it can serve as a mechanism for injustice, particularly when parties lack the resources to mount a robust defense against such motions. The implications of a Summary Judgment extend beyond mere procedural efficiency; they can significantly impact the lives of individuals involved, often determining the outcome of their legal battles without the benefit of a trial. This raises critical questions about fairness and equity in the legal system, particularly for those who may not have the means to adequately defend themselves.

Subsequent Interactions with Legal Counsel

Following the initial shock of receiving the Summary Judgment notification, the next phase typically involves engaging with legal counsel to navigate the implications of the ruling. This interaction is crucial, as it provides an opportunity for the litigant to gain clarity regarding the legal landscape and the potential avenues for recourse. The role of legal counsel in this context cannot be overstated; they serve as the navigators of the often turbulent waters of the legal system, providing guidance and support to their clients.

During these discussions, it is common for clients to express feelings of frustration and confusion, seeking reassurance from their attorneys regarding the validity of the judgment and the possibility of appeal. Legal counsel, in turn, must balance the emotional needs of their clients with the objective realities of the case. This necessitates a nuanced approach, wherein attorneys must not only elucidate the legal principles at play but also provide empathetic support to clients grappling with the emotional fallout of the judgment.

Moreover, the attorney-client relationship during this period can significantly influence the litigant's emotional recovery. A compassionate attorney who takes the time to listen and validate their client's feelings can help mitigate some of the distress associated with the ruling. This supportive dynamic can empower clients, enabling them to approach the next steps with a clearer mind and renewed determination.

Emotional and Social Ramifications

The emotional ramifications of receiving a Summary Judgment notification extend far beyond the immediate shock of the ruling. Individuals often experience a profound sense of loss, as the dismissal of their case may signify the culmination of months or even years of effort and investment in pursuing justice. This sense of loss can manifest in various ways, including feelings of inadequacy, anger, and despair. Furthermore, the psychological toll of navigating the legal system can exacerbate existing mental health issues, leading to increased anxiety and stress.

Moreover, the social implications of a Summary Judgment can be equally significant. Individuals may find themselves isolated from their support networks, as the stigma associated with legal disputes can lead to feelings of shame and embarrassment. This isolation can further compound the emotional distress experienced by litigants, creating a vicious cycle that is difficult to escape. Friends and family may not fully understand the complexities of the situation, leading to a lack of support when it is needed most.

Additionally, the long-term emotional effects can linger well beyond the immediate aftermath of the ruling. Individuals may develop a pervasive distrust of the legal system, feeling that their voices were not heard or that justice was not served.

This disillusionment can impact their willingness to engage in future legal matters, potentially deterring them from seeking justice in other areas of their lives.

The complexities of the legal system present significant challenges for litigants, particularly those who are not well-versed in legal principles. The intricacies of procedural rules, coupled with the often-opaque nature of legal terminology, can create barriers to understanding and effectively navigating the judicial process. This is particularly pronounced in cases involving Summary Judgment, where the stakes are high, and the consequences of misunderstanding can be dire.

Furthermore, the disparity in resources between parties can exacerbate these challenges. Litigants who lack access to competent legal representation may find themselves at a distinct disadvantage as they struggle to comprehend the nuances of their case and the implications of the Summary Judgment ruling. This inequity highlights the importance of access to justice and the need for systemic reforms to ensure that all individuals, regardless of their financial means, can effectively advocate for their rights.

Moreover, the procedural complexities can lead to a sense of alienation among litigants. Many individuals may feel overwhelmed by the legal process, leading to disengagement and a lack of agency in their own cases. This sense of powerlessness can further exacerbate the emotional toll of legal disputes, making it imperative for legal systems to prioritize transparency and accessibility.

Considering the emotional and systemic challenges associated with Summary Judgment, the importance of effective legal representation cannot be overstated. Competent attorneys play a critical role in advocating their clients' interests, ensuring that their voices are heard and their rights are protected. This advocacy extends beyond mere legal representation; it encompasses a holistic approach that addresses the emotional and psychological needs of clients as they navigate the complexities of the legal system.

Moreover, effective representation can significantly impact the outcome of a case. Attorneys who are well-versed in the intricacies of Summary Judgment motions can identify potential weaknesses in the opposing party's arguments, thereby positioning their clients for a more favorable outcome. This underscores the necessity for litigants to seek out qualified legal counsel who can provide the expertise and support needed to navigate the complexities of the judicial process.

Additionally, the role of legal representation extends to educating clients about their rights and options. A knowledgeable attorney can empower clients by providing them with the information they need to make informed decisions about their cases. This empowerment can help mitigate feelings of helplessness and foster a sense of agency, which is crucial for emotional recovery following a Summary Judgment ruling.

Reflecting on the Implications of Summary Judgment

In conclusion, the experience of receiving a Summary Judgment notification is fraught with emotional and practical implications that extend far beyond the immediate legal context. The initial shock of the ruling, coupled with the subsequent interactions with legal counsel, highlights the multifaceted nature of navigating the legal system. Furthermore, the systemic challenges faced by litigants underscore the importance of access to effective representation in ensuring that justice is served.

Ultimately, the implications of Summary Judgment extend beyond the individual litigants involved; they reflect broader societal issues related to access to justice, the equitable treatment of parties within the legal system, and the need for ongoing reforms to address these disparities. By fostering a deeper understanding of these complexities, we can work towards a more just and equitable legal system that serves the interests of all individuals, regardless of their circumstances.

It is essential that we advocate for changes that enhance transparency, accessibility, and fairness in the legal process, ensuring that no one is left to navigate these turbulent waters alone.

The art of legal advocacy is a nuanced and complex endeavor, requiring a deep understanding of both the law and human psychology. Throughout the trial, the attorneys meticulously crafted their arguments, weaving together facts, testimonies, and legal precedents to create a compelling narrative that would resonate with a jury or, in this case, the judge. This process involved not only the presentation of evidence but also the ability to anticipate and counter the opposing counsel's arguments. The attorneys' ability to synthesize complex legal concepts into accessible language was crucial in ensuring that the jurors could grasp the intricacies of the case.

Moreover, the emotional intelligence displayed by the attorneys in connecting with the jury was equally important; they needed to evoke empathy and understanding while maintaining the integrity of their arguments. This delicate balance was essential in persuading the jury to see the case through their lens.

The Emotional Landscape of the Hearing

While the hearing was fundamentally a legal proceeding, it was also an emotional journey for all involved. The testimonies presented in court were often deeply personal, revealing the profound impact of the events in question on the lives of the individuals involved.

The judges tasked with evaluating these narratives were not immune to the emotional weight of the testimonies. Their ability to remain objective while grappling with the emotional realities of the case was a testament to their commitment to justice.

In examining the multifaceted experiences and challenges faced by Geraldine Taylor during her tenure at the Gary Job Corps Center, it becomes imperative to delve into the intricate dynamics of workplace stress, management practices, and the implications of decision-making power within an organizational context. The narrative of Geraldine's professional journey serves as a poignant case study that elucidates the broader themes of burnout, emotional exhaustion, and the detrimental effects of inadequate leadership. This analysis systematically explores the various dimensions of her experiences, particularly focusing on the period from April 2004 to November 2005, a time marked by significant personal and professional turmoil. By understanding these dynamics, insights can be gained into how similar organizations might better support their employees and fulfill their missions.

CHAPTER THIRTY-ONE: EMOTIONAL EXHAUSTION

The condition characterized by emotional exhaustion, depersonalization, and a diminished sense of personal accomplishment was particularly evident in Geraldine's narrative. Throughout her time at the Gary Job Corps Center, she faced excessive stress that eventually culminated in profound emotional fatigue. This state was worsened by the lack of intervention from senior management in addressing pervasive employment discrimination issues within the workplace environment. The absence of proactive measures not only contributed to Geraldine's physical and mental exhaustion but also fostered a culture of silence and fear among the staff.

After six meetings with the first attorney and five court appearances for preliminary hearings and attorney arguments before the judge, the emotional toll of exhaustion was compounded by the feeling of being trapped in a toxic work environment. The lack of support from management often left employees with a sense of helplessness. In Geraldine's case, senior management's failure to acknowledge and rectify discriminatory practices created an atmosphere where employees felt undervalued and marginalized. This neglect not only impacted individual well-being but also had far-reaching implications for team cohesion and overall organizational effectiveness.

The pervasive nature of these issues often led to a cycle of disengagement. Employees, including Geraldine, began to withdraw from their roles, further worsening the challenges faced by the organization.

Denial of Decision-Making Power

Another critical aspect of Geraldine's experience at the Gary Job Corps Center was the systematic denial of her decision-making power, despite her extensive knowledge and skills honed over a remarkable 29-year career. This denial undermined her professional autonomy and contributed to a pervasive sense of frustration and disillusionment. Geraldine was in a tough situation.

When individuals can't use their skills and aren't given a voice, it significantly affects their overall well-being and productivity. *Why can't they see what I bring to the table?* she thought. Creating an environment that values and utilizes each team member's expertise is crucial for both personal and organizational success.

The ramifications of this denial extended beyond Geraldine's individual experience. It significantly impacted the cohesiveness of the Wellness Center staff. As fear of job loss and retaliation from management loomed large, the collaborative spirit essential for effective teamwork began to erode. The staff, once united in their mission to support the youth at the Job Corps Center, found themselves operating in a climate of mistrust and anxiety. This deterioration of relationships not only affected morale but also compromised the quality of services provided to the center's participants, undermining the organization's mission.

The absence of empowerment in the workplace had a profound impact on employees' motivation and engagement. When team members feel undervalued and unable to contribute meaningfully, it often results in a disengaged workforce that merely goes through the motions rather than actively striving to achieve the organization's goals. Addressing this issue could involve creating opportunities for employees to voice their ideas, encouraging participation in decision-making processes, and recognizing and rewarding contributions. By fostering a more inclusive and empowering environment, organizations can unlock the full potential of their workforce.

Inexperienced Management and Poor Leadership

The challenges faced by Geraldine were further exacerbated by inexperienced management, particularly under the leadership of individuals such as Phyllis Smith and Carol Benson. Their lack of familiarity with the Job Corps environment and the unique challenges it presented led to decision-making processes that were often disconnected from the realities faced by staff and participants.

The imposition of directives without soliciting input from experienced personnel alienated the staff and led to widespread non-compliance with policies that were ill-conceived and poorly communicated. This disconnect created a chasm between management and staff, where the latter felt their voices were not valued, leading to increased frustration and disengagement.

This breakdown in communication and leadership was emblematic of a broader issue within organizational structures. Ineffective leadership often triggers a cascade of negative outcomes, including disengagement, low morale, and diminished organizational effectiveness.

In Geraldine's situation, the forced adherence to the directives of inexperienced management created an environment where innovation and best practices were stifled. The staff, feeling disempowered and undervalued, became less likely to engage in proactive problem-solving or advocate for the needs of the youth they served. Consequently, the overall effectiveness of the Gary Job Corps Center was jeopardized, as the potential for growth and improvement was systematically undermined by poor leadership. The absence of mentorship and guidance from experienced leaders further compounded the challenges faced by the staff, leaving them without the necessary support to navigate their roles effectively.

The Interplay of Stressors and Their Consequences

The interplay of these stressors—burnout, denial of decision-making power, and inexperienced management—created a perfect storm that significantly impacted Geraldine's professional life. The cumulative effect of these challenges manifested not only in her emotional and physical well-being but also in her professional identity.

As she grappled with the realities of her situation, the once-fulfilling aspects of her career became overshadowed by the stressors that permeated her daily experiences. The joy and passion that initially drew her to the field began to wane, replaced by a sense of dread and disillusionment.

Moreover, the consequences of these stressors extended beyond the individual level, affecting the organizational culture and the quality of services provided to the youth at the center. When staff members were subjected to high levels of stress and felt disenfranchised, the ripple effects led to increased turnover rates, decreased productivity, and a decline in overall workforce morale.

This cycle of negativity not only hampered the effectiveness of the organization but also posed significant challenges to the mission of empowering and supporting the youth who relied on the services provided by the Job Corps Center. The lack of a supportive environment deterred potential talent from joining the organization, perpetuating the cycle of dysfunction and discontent.

Implications for Organizational Change

Considering Geraldine's experiences, it became evident that there was a pressing need for organizational change within the Gary Job Corps Center. Addressing the root causes of burnout and emotional exhaustion required a multifaceted approach that prioritized employee well-being, fostered a culture of open communication, and empowered staff to participate in decision-making processes.

Furthermore, the development of leadership training programs aimed at equipping managers with the necessary skills to navigate the complexities of the Job Corps environment was essential for fostering a supportive and effective workplace. Such training could include mentorship opportunities, conflict resolution strategies, and techniques for fostering inclusivity and collaboration among staff.

Implementing mechanisms to address employment discrimination and promote inclusivity within the organization was also crucial for creating a safe and supportive environment for all employees. By actively engaging in practices that promoted equity and fairness, management could begin to rebuild trust and restore morale among the staff, ultimately enhancing the quality of services provided to the youth. Regular feedback sessions, anonymous reporting mechanisms, and diversity training could serve as foundational steps toward creating a more equitable workplace.

These initiatives would not only benefit the employees but also enhance the overall effectiveness of the organization in fulfilling its mission.

The Beautiful Sky View of San Marcos, Texas

The experiences and challenges faced by Geraldine Taylor at the Gary Job Corps Center served as a compelling case study that highlighted the intricate dynamics of workplace stress, management practices, and the implications of decision-making power within an organizational context. The interplay of burnout, denial of agency, and poor leadership not only impacted Geraldine's professional identity but also had far-reaching consequences for the organizational culture and the quality of services provided to the youth.

As such, it was imperative for organizations to recognize the significance of fostering a supportive and empowering work environment where employees were valued, heard, and equipped to contribute meaningfully to the mission at hand.

The lessons learned from Geraldine's narrative underscored the necessity for systemic change, ultimately paving the way for a more resilient and effective organizational framework that prioritized the well-being of both employees and the individuals they served. By addressing these critical issues, organizations could not only improve employee satisfaction and retention but also enhance their overall impact on the communities they served.

Following the devastating blow of a summary judgment rendered by the U.S. District Court for the Western District of Texas, a profound sense of disillusionment permeated Geraldine's experience. This was largely exacerbated by the lackluster representation provided by her attorney, Chris Pattard. Considering this unsatisfactory legal counsel, Geraldine resolved to pursue an appeal with the Fifth Circuit Court of Appeals, undertaking this endeavor *pro se,* which necessitated a considerable degree of self-reliance and legal acumen.

Concurrently, she filed a second complaint with the Equal Employment Opportunity Commission (EEOC), augmenting her initial allegations with new charges that she believed warranted further examination.

CHAPTER THIRTY-TWO: IMPLICATIONS OF THE DISCUSSION

The character of Geraldine serves as a powerful representation of the intersection between healthcare and social rehabilitation, highlighting the critical role that dedicated professionals play in the lives of those they serve. Her presence in the infirmary not only provided essential medical care but also fostered a sense of hope and security among the students. The apprehension felt by the narrator regarding Geraldine's safety underscored broader societal concerns about the well-being of healthcare providers in high-stress environments, illuminating the urgent need for systemic changes that prioritized their protection.

Furthermore, the personal struggles faced by the narrator enriched the narrative, reflecting the universal challenges encountered in the pursuit of aspirations. Ultimately, this exploration of Geraldine's role and the surrounding dynamics served to illuminate the profound impact of healthcare professionals on individual lives and the necessity of supporting those who dedicate themselves to such vital work.

In examining Geraldine's multifaceted character and professional trajectory, it became evident that her ability to compartmentalize her emotions not only served as a coping mechanism but also as a catalyst for her personal and professional growth. This nuanced approach to her responsibilities allowed her to navigate the complexities of her dual roles with remarkable efficacy.

Furthermore, the ritualistic sharing of daily experiences with her family not only provided a therapeutic outlet but also reinforced the significance of familial solidarity in the face of external adversities. Geraldine's even-mindedness, characterized by her quiet yet perceptive nature, reflected a profound understanding of the dynamics within her work environment. By consciously choosing to remain uninvolved in the personal affairs of her colleagues, she adeptly maintained her reputation as a diligent and principled worker, which, in turn, fortified her standing within both her professional and domestic spheres.

Despite the systemic challenges she faced, including being consistently overlooked and underpaid, her unwavering commitment to the Job Corps program exemplified a significant dedication to her vocation. The transformative journey that Geraldine undertook over the course of five years was emblematic of resilience and the pursuit of excellence.

As she evolved into a master of her craft as a medical technician, her ascent to leadership roles — such as wellness center shift leader and center pregnancy coordinator — underscored her capacity for growth and adaptation. This trajectory not only highlighted her professional achievements but also served as a testament to the profound impact of perseverance in overcoming institutional barriers. Consequently, Geraldine's story resonated as an inspiring narrative of empowerment, illustrating how individual agency could flourish amidst systemic challenges.

Takeaway

This tumultuous period ignited within Geraldine a renewed determination to meticulously craft a compelling case, one that could potentially attract the attention of a more competent attorney, despite her uncertainty regarding the appropriate legal representation to seek. *How do I find someone who can truly help?* she wondered.

The summary judgment, rather than extinguishing her resolve, served as a catalyst for action, instilling a fervent desire to advocate for her rights and seek justice in a system that often appeared indifferent to the plight of individuals. Thus, the journey toward reclaiming agency in the face of adversity commenced, characterized by a commitment to navigating the complexities of the legal landscape with renewed vigor and purpose.

SONG LYRIC – BALLARD OF GERALDINE

"ATTRIBUTE"

[Verse]

Geraldine got a heart of gold, pure and bright

Faced abuse got caught in the night

Dark hearts with iron hands took her soul

Left her standing out in the cold

[Verse 2]

Shame of lies wrapped around her tight

Corruption turned her days into nights

Experienced with cruel dark eyes

Left Geraldine fighting endless cries

[Chorus]

We sing for Geraldine, who stood so tall

Even when the world tried to make her fall

No more tears for the dark, cruel past

In our memories, Geraldine will last

[Verse 3]

Through the storm, she walked, battle-scarred feet

Found the strength in her chest to beat

Loneliness, a shadow she knew too well

But she rose from the depths, broke the spell

[Verse 4]

Streets whisper tales of her silent scream

Rivers ran dry with her broken dreams

Yet she painted hope where the grey skies hung

Geraldine's anthem, forever sung

[Chorus]

We sing for Geraldine, who stood so tall

Even when the world tried to make her fall

No more tears for the dark, cruel past

In our memories, Geraldine will last

[Verse]

Geraldine got a heart of gold, pure and bright

Faced abuse got caught in the night

Dark hearts with iron hands took her soul

Left her standing out in the cold

Dedicated To Geraldine Taylor With Love

[Verse 2]

Shame of lies wrapped around her tight

Corruption turned her days into nights

Experienced with cruel dark eyes

Left Geraldine fighting endless cries

[Chorus]

We sing for Geraldine, who stood so tall

Even when the world tried to make her fall

No more tears for the dark, cruel past

In our memories, Geraldine will last

[Verse 3]

Through the storm, she walked, battle-scarred feet

Found the strength in her chest to beat

Loneliness, a shadow she knew too well

But she rose from the depths, broke the spell

[Verse 4]

Streets whisper tales of her silent scream

Rivers ran dry with her broken dreams

Yet she painted hope where the grey skies hung

Geraldine's anthem, forever sung

[Chorus]

We sing for Geraldine, who stood so tall

Even when the world tried to make her fall

No more tears for the dark, cruel past

In our memories, Geraldine will last

Written Lyrics and Music Composed By Arthur Taylor With Love

ABOUT THE AUTHOR

Arthur Taylor

[Photo provided by Michael Taylor]

Arthur's life narrative, originating from the historic small city of Brenham, Texas, is emblematic of the complexities and challenges faced by individuals navigating the intersection of personal adversity and societal expectations. This story critically examines the formative experiences that shaped Arthur's trajectory, particularly focusing on his early education, work in mortuary science, and subsequent military service, all of which contribute to a nuanced understanding of his character and the thematic undercurrents present in his literary work, particularly in *Dark Hearts Iron Hands - The Conspiracy.*

Early Life and Educational Challenges

Born in a city renowned for its historical significance as the birthplace of Texas, Arthur's upbringing in a single-family home alongside six siblings undoubtedly instilled in him a profound sense of familial responsibility and resilience. His educational journey commenced at Brenham Independent Schools, where he attended classes up to the tenth grade. However, the challenges he faced were compounded by a learning disability, which ultimately led to his decision to drop out of school. This pivotal moment, characterized by a sense of regret and introspection, marked the beginning of a tumultuous period in Arthur's life. The realization that abandoning his education was a significant misstep catalyzed a profound desire for change, prompting him to seek alternative avenues for personal and professional growth.

Work Experience in Mortuary Science

During his high school years, Arthur's engagement with the local funeral home as an understudy in mortuary science provided him with invaluable life lessons and insights into the human condition. This experience, which encompassed a range of responsibilities—from preparing funerals to assisting in ambulance services—not only honed his practical skills but also deepened his understanding of mortality and the rituals surrounding death. The exposure to such profound themes at a young age undoubtedly influenced his literary voice, allowing him to explore complex emotional landscapes in his writing. Furthermore, the juxtaposition of his youthful aspirations against the backdrop of his work in funeral home services is a poignant metaphor for the struggles between hope and despair, a recurring motif in *Dark Hearts Iron Hands - The Conspiracy.*

Military Service and Personal Transformation

After a brief stint in the job market, during which Arthur grappled with the consequences of his educational decisions, he made the consequential choice to enlist in the United States Army. This decision marked a significant turning point in his life, as military service provided him with structure, discipline, and a renewed sense of purpose. The Army not only facilitated his personal transformation but also equipped him with the skills necessary to navigate the complexities of adult life. The experiences garnered during his service, including exposure to diverse perspectives and the cultivation of leadership qualities, further enriched his narrative voice, allowing him to synthesize his past struggles with newfound autonomy and resilience.

The Implications of Arthur's Journey

Arthur's life story is a testament to the profound impact of early experiences on personal development and artistic expression. His journey—from a challenging upbringing in Brenham, Texas, through the trials of educational setbacks and the transformative power of military service—culminates in a rich tapestry of themes explored in *Dark Hearts Iron Hands - The Conspiracy.* The interplay of regret, resilience, and the quest for meaning within human experience resonates deeply within his work, inviting readers to engage with the complexities of existence.

Ultimately, Arthur's narrative serves as a compelling reminder of the significance of education, the value of personal growth, and the enduring power of storytelling as a means of understanding the human condition. The narrative poignantly captures this struggle, illustrating how the fear for Geraldine's safety resonates not only with the narrator but also with the community at large, thereby emphasizing the urgent need for systemic changes that prioritize the protection and support of healthcare workers.

Personal Struggles and Broader Challenges

As the narrative unfolds, it becomes increasingly evident that the struggles faced by the narrator—balancing the demands of marriage, education, and financial instability—are reflective of the broader challenges that many individuals encounter in their pursuit of aspirations. This personal struggle enriches the narrative, serving to humanize the experience of those involved in the healthcare system. The complexities of navigating personal and professional responsibilities underscore the multifaceted nature of life in high-stress environments, where the pursuit of one's goals is often fraught with obstacles. Moreover, the narrator's journey resonates with a universal audience, as it encapsulates the trials and tribulations that many individuals face in their quest for stability and fulfillment.

In the case of Taylor V. Management Training d/b\a/Gary Job Corps Center, it is hereby ordering

Summary Judgement in favor of the Defense

Dark Hearts-Iron Hands "The Conspiracy."

This Court Stands Adjourned

Part One

REFERENCES

Merriam-Webster. (n.d.). Depersonalization. In Merriam-Webster.com dictionary. Retrieved from https://www.merriam-webster.com/sentences/depersonalization

Edge Foundation. (n.d.). How working memory impairments can shape emotional responses in ADHD. Retrieved from https://edgefoundation.org/how-working-memory-impairments-can-shapeemotional-responses-in-adhd/ Language. (n.d.). Legal matters. Retrieved from https://lawguage.com/category/legal-matters/page/3/

Esquire. (2023, November 30). Arkansas Law School 1L study guide for civil procedure. Law School Outlines. Retrieved from https://marketguest.com/simplifying-the-turkey-visa-process-for-sri-lankantravelers/

The Garza Firm. (n.d.). California race discrimination lawyer. Retrieved from https://www.thegarzafirm.com/california-race-discrimination-lawyer/

Decision Makers Hub. (n.d.). 3 empathetic strategies to improve employee engagement and retention. Retrieved from https://decisionmakershub.com/3empathetic-strategies-to-improve-employee-engagement-and-retention/

Black Success Today. (n.d.). Pride ROC Chicago. Retrieved from https://blacksuccesstoday.com/blogs/blacknews/priderocchicago

Fiverr Blog. (2023, November). What is a multi-geo-enabled tenant, and how it works? Retrieved from https://fiverr1403.blogspot.com/2023/11/what-is-multigeo-enabled-tenant-and.html NYSIADA. (n.d.). Companies. Retrieved from https://nysiada.org/uncategorized/companies/

Vikki Wiki. (n.d.). Be bothered. Retrieved from https://vikki.wiki/be-bothered/

MGLSA. (n.d.). Feature. Retrieved from https://www.mglsa.com/feature/

Flipp Advertising. (n.d.). Collaborating with an enneagram 6: Embracing the guardian. Retrieved from https://flippadvertising.com/news/collaboratingwith-an-enneagram-6-embracing-the-guardian/

Net Reputation. (n.d.). The power and impact of propaganda. Retrieved from https://www.netreputation.com/the-power-and-impact-of-propaganda/

Commercial Law Solicitors. (n.d.). Reporting harassment and discrimination: Employee rights and protections. Retrieved from https://commercial-lawsolicitors.co.uk/reporting-harassment-and-discrimination-employee-rightsand-protections-1

Bassanova. (n.d.). Chelsea initiates disciplinary measures against Enzo Fernandez amid racist video controversy. Retrieved from

https://bassanova.co.za/chelsea-initiates-disciplinary-measures-against-enzofernandez-amid-racist-video-controversy/

Equanimity Wellbeing. (n.d.). Rates and insurance. Retrieved from https://www.equanimitywellbeing.org/rates-and-insurance

Inclusivv. (n.d.). Understanding microaggressions: How small actions can have a big impact. Retrieved from https://www.inclusivv.co/blog/understandingmicroaggressions-how-small-actions-can-have-a-big-impact

Blog Chatter. (n.d.). Understanding bullying, bossing, and mobbing in the workplace: Impacts and prevention strategies. Retrieved from https://www.theblogchatter.com/blogrolls/understanding-bullying-bossingand-mobbing-in-the-workplace-impacts-and-prevention-strategies-pebblesgalaxy

Collaborate Advocate Navigate. (n.d.). Special education history. Retrieved from https://collaborateadvocatenavigate.org/parents-can/special-educationhistory/

RCF. (n.d.). About: Chairman. Retrieved from

https://rcf.org.pk/About/Chairman

Natural Justice. (n.d.). Press release: Civil society in court to challenge gas power plant in Richards Bay. Retrieved from https://naturaljustice.org/pressrelease-civil-society-in-court-to-challenge-gas-power-plant-in-richards-bay/ Swift Feed. (n.d.). Challenges refugees encounter. Retrieved from https://swiftfeed.news/challenges-refugees-encounter/

Arab City Schools. (n.d.). Retrieved from

https://www.arabcityschools.org/apps/pages/index.jsp?uREC_ID=3766 593=d_ID=2442328

Rent Boca Offices. (n.d.). Types of workplace discrimination. Retrieved from https://rentbocaoffices.com/types-workplace-discrimination/

Valued Moves. (n.d.). Commercial clearances. Retrieved from https://valuedmoves.co.uk/commercial-clearances/

MNK Lawyers. (n.d.). Lessons learned from employment law litigation. Retrieved from https://mnklawyers.com/lessons-learned-from-employmentlaw-litigation/

LN Trial Lawyers. (n.d.). What steps can you take to address sexual harassment at work? Retrieved from https://lntriallawyers.com/blog/what-steps-can-youtake-to-address-sexual-harassment-at-work/

The Bib Theorists. (n.d.). The Bib Theorists: Uncovering the truth about the father of modern gynecology. Retrieved from https://thebibtheorists.com/thebib-theorists-uncovering-the-truth-about-the-father-of-modern-gynecology/

Hogo Next. (n.d.). How to address and combat workplace discrimination. Retrieved from https://hogonext.com/how-to-address-and-combat-workplacediscrimination/

www.ingramcontent.com/pod-product-compliance
Lightning Source LLC
Chambersburg PA
CBHW060401310726
48976CB00003B/898